Operation: Save Santa

D.T. Ihaza

To Helen
best wishes!

First Published in 2019 by The Manuscript Publisher

ISBN: 978-1-911442-22-6

A CIP Catalogue record for this book is available from the National Library

Front cover illustration by Conor Carton

Cover design by Karolina Smorczewska

Typesetting, page design and layout by DocumentsandManuscripts.com

Published, printed and bound in Ireland

Operation: Save Santa

Contents

CHAPTER 1

A Wish

'It is going to be a very cold winter,' according to the weatherman but then, that's what they always say about winter in Ireland. Well, you just never know.

It was definitely a cold night tonight. It was also the day that changed my opinion on fantasy, fairy tales, leprechauns and, the big guy with the white beard. You know, the one who lives in the North Pole and wears a red suit.

I woke up quite early this morning, in a snow-capped cottage. It was so cold that I could breathe frost around the room. My three brothers – Ronan, Liam and James – were snoring their heads off. They sounded like the three little pigs, all grunting and snorting. I thought the vibrations would make the snow fall off the roof but, there was no avalanche today.

I gazed out the foggy glass window, at the snow-covered fields. The sun was trying to break through the thick smog of cloud and mist. It looked as if it was shining down, its rays trying to seek help.

Well, if it was looking for my help, all I could do was to say a prayer. In Ireland, that is the answer. If someone dies in the family, I'll say a prayer for you. If someone is ill, I'll say a prayer for you and so on. The sun was certain to get my prayers today, for one reason and one reason only – I was stuck to the cold floor. My two feet were more like concrete blocks and the frost was the cement.

"Ronan Joseph O'Reilly, if you don't give me back my socks this instant, I will see that Jenny Murphy hears all about you wearing your sisters' pink woolly socks to bed," I screamed at the top of my voice.

"Alright, calm down, you can have your woolly socks back Miss Queen of Sheba," Ronan replied wearily.

"Thank you and it's Ms Shelia to you," I snapped back.

Yes, that's me, Ms. Sheila O'Reilly, the eldest of my family, followed by my three brothers. Although I am the eldest, unfortunately, I have to share my birthday with my twin brother, Ronan. We were both born on the 25th of December. We were going to be 16 on Saturday, which also happened to be Christmas Day. I was so excited.

"Shelia, Shelia, are Mammy and Daddy back yet? Is it Christmas Day? Can we make a snowman? What's for breakfast?" James being the gabby one in the family.

"Alright, take a breath, Baby James. So many questions for such a tiny leprechaun," I tried talking to him in the only language he understood.

"No Shelia, I'm not a leprechaun anymore. Today, I am an elf," James said proudly.

"Well, that's perfect timing. I'm sure Santa Claus will need your help in the North Pole," I continued with the pretence.

"Will you stop encouraging him?" Ronan said with his teeth chattering with the cold. Well that and the fact that he now had no socks to keep him warm.

"Sure, it isn't me! It's Mammy who fills his head with stories of superheroes and what-not," I said in my defence.

"Ah, that may be but, you still call him Baby James when he is five years old," Ronan replied smugly.

So, I stuck out my tongue at him. I know it was childish but, I had no come back.

I still call James, Baby James because Mammy used to call him that when we were younger and, I guess it just stuck with me. It kind of rolls off my tongue without me even noticing.

"Alright, you little elf, let's go to the kitchen and Shelia will make you some porridge to warm you up before your hard-working day ahead."

"Do you really think Santa has loads of elves making toys in the North Pole?" James asks me in that innocent voice of his.

"Yeah ... sure. Would you like some jam on your porridge?" I said, trying to change the topic of conversation.

I can't say I ever grasped the idea of Santa Claus and the delivering of presents on a sleigh on Christmas Eve. I guess, I have always been a more serious type of girl. I remember my mother telling me fairy-tales about mythical creatures called unicorns but, I guess I was more of a tomboy. Tomboy was the word we used to describe girls that liked sports and climbing trees rather than playing mammies with dolls. Today was going to be the day when, everything I thought was black and white, was going to become green, red and sparkly.

"What day is it?" Liam said as he was dragging his feet across the kitchen floor and wiping the sleep from his eyes.

"Well, good afternoon to you too, Liam. Did you have a nice sleep?" I greeted him. "It's Saturday, the 18th of December and, it is half past twelve in the afternoon."

It was a very cold morning, with snow on the rooftops and the fields. Then, it hit me like a hot Irish stew Mammy would make for Sunday dinner. I should have known he wasn't well but, I just thought, 'Typical Liam'. He would sleep all day and night if you let him. In winter, Mammy would always say, 'Liam is gone into hibernation'. She would always talk about how some animals would gather food and go for a long sleep during winter. Well, one thing is for sure, Liam didn't gather the food but instead, he just ate too much, woke up from his long sleep and vomited all over my pink, woolly socks. Cringe!

I checked his temperature and he was a little on the hot side. I jokingly told him, "You could fry an Irish breakfast on you."

I was trying to get a smile out of him but, it only made him vomit more. Ok, so maybe 'full Irish breakfast' were not the most comforting words he needed to hear but, what did I know? Trust Mammy and Daddy to go to Dublin a week before Christmas. Now, I was left playing the role of Mammy.

"Are you okay now, Liam?" I asked, hoping that I wouldn't throw up.

"I want Mammy," Liam sighed.

"I know but, Mammy will be home tomorrow and, she's going to bring us all lovely presents and some adventure stories from the city and, well eh ...!"

(I thought to myself, That's it; I am all out of ideas.)

"So, what's going on in here? Whoa! Stop!" I yelled at the top of my voice.

Before the words even left my mouth, Ronan was flat out on the floor. He had slipped on Liam's spew and hurt his back.

For a brief moment, I remember saying to myself, If there is a Santa living in the North Pole, with loads of elves, I wish he would take me to live with him?

Now that's a wish I never thought would come true

Chapter 2
A Bedtime Story

It was a long day looking after a sick brother, an injured brother and a little elf. As Saturday evening came closer, the Great Chill began to return. I could feel the sharp nip of frost in the air, the roof was sparkling with ice and the sun had gone back in behind the night-time clouds.

"Tell us a story about Santa and the elves," said Baby James.

"Ok but, after your bath and you are in your pyjamas. Then I will tell you a bedtime story."

"About Santa and the elves?" exclaimed James with excitement.

"Yes," I said. (What was I thinking? Me! Tell a story! About Santa and his elves!)

"Well, this is going to be great," Ronan said laughingly, forgetting about his sore back as he jumped up on the chair. "Ah my back!" he shouted in agony.

"Well, serves you right for laughing. I've got Mammy's genes. Besides, I read books so, how hard could it be?" I said confidently.

It was now seven o' clock. The night time had set in. The black sky was clear with only the stars twinkling and the moon beamed down over the cottage. I knew the time was coming for me to entertain Liam, James and now, Ronan, with my bedtime story.

As the clock ticked, my heart beat faster. The sweat was rolling off my brow while I tried to give James a bath. Then, you wouldn't believe it! That stupid cuckoo clock, which Daddy bought for Mammy at the Sunday market, started chirping. It was eight o'clock and time for my performance.

As the boys were now settled into bed and Liam's temperature had gone down, it was time for ... The Story. So, I began with the usual "once upon a time" (that's what I could remember from the fairy-tale books). "It was a very cold winter." (Thank you, weatherman, for those great words.) "It was Christmas Eve. Santa Claus and his elves were getting the toys ready for delivery."

"Yawn, I'm bored already," interrupted Ronan.

"Will you shush? I'm just setting the scene," I snapped.

"When you said a bedtime story, you really meant it. Where's the joy and the excitement? It's Christmas and I'm already dozing off." Ronan continued to get on my nerves.

"Oh! So, you would like to take over my boring story? Be my guest!" I gestured.

"No, no! I'll be shutting up now," Ronan replied sheepishly.

"Thank you. Now the elves were helping Santa load his big heavy bag onto his sleigh."

"What toys did he have?" James interrupted now. "Well you know: bikes, cars, teddy bears and dolls for the girls," said James.

"And dolls for the girls," I replied. "Well, like I said, it was a cold winter and Santa decided that he should wear extra woolly socks for his journey."

"What colour were they?" asked Ronan.

"They were red and green and very sparkly," I answered. "Does that sound exciting to you, Ronan or, do you only prefer pink? Now I know what to buy you for Christmas."

James giggled and whispered to Liam, "Shelia is going to buy Ronan pink woolly socks for Christmas."

"Oh, well I'm glad you're enjoying the story," I said to James.

Liam looked a lot better as he sat up listening to the banter between myself and Ronan.

"Shelia, can I have some warm milk?" Liam asked in a happier tone.

"Of course. As long as you don't throw up on me again," I scolded him with a wink.

"Sheila! Do you know how you're my favourite sister in the whole world?" Ronan said, attempting to flatter me.

"I'll get some for everyone but, you better all stay in bed because, the fire is nearly out in the kitchen and we need to stay warm."

When I left for the kitchen, I was delighted. I got a break from the story which, to be honest, was even beginning to bore me!

I took the carton of milk from the fridge and placed it on the counter. I took a saucepan from the cupboard and put it on the range. I was hoping there would be enough heat from the coals to warm the milk, so I wouldn't have to use the gas.

As I was standing over the range, I got a feeling down my spine. Kind of tingly, like magic. Then I thought, it was probably just the cold. For the first time, I think the weatherman was right. There was something about this winter that just felt unbearable.

I poured half of the carton of milk into the saucepan and returned it to the fridge. I then took some sugar from the tin to add to the milk, just to give it a little extra sweetness. (*Well, it is Christmas*, I thought.)

When I was finished with the sugar, I once again felt that same chill down my back. It made my whole body shiver. It was almost like I was a snowman, standing outside during a snowstorm. Then I felt it. That tiny touch that would change my life forever. It was like a bird using his beak to peck at a piece of bread.

I brushed away at my neck, thinking it was a spider or a fly but then, it was at my leg. Something was pulling on my dressing gown. I thought it was one of the boys playing a trick on me. As I turned around to scold him, I was looking into mid-air but then, I looked down. There it was – a small creature about the same height as a hamster. It had a pointy nose, red flushed cheeks, high peaked ears and a skinny body. It wore green clothes and a pointed hat.

That was it, I had fallen asleep. My story was so boring that I was now dreaming about seeing an elf. Of course, by the end of this cold winter's night, I wished it had been a dream. I could then go back to being Shelia O'Reilly from Castlebar, Co. Mayo, who loves bossing her brothers around and wearing pink woolly socks but tonight, that was not the case. It was all real. There was an elf in my kitchen. I needed to sit down for this.

"Hello there! I didn't mean to startle you. My name is Buddy and I was listening to your story about Santa. You were doing really well only ..."

"Only?" I said in utter dismay at what I was seeing in front of me. (*I'm going to wake up now and it's all a dream and that's that. Elves are a myth, Santa is a myth*, I said to myself over and over.)

"Excuse me!" Buddy interrupted my rambling thoughts. "Your milk is boiling over!"

"Oh no! Ouch I've burnt myself. The boys are still waiting for their milk and I'm standing here talking to an elf. That's it: I'm delirious and I must have caught Liam's illness."

"No, you're not sick Sheila. I really am an elf, in your kitchen and you probably want to put your hand under a cold tap."

"Thanks ... I think. So, what do ...? How do you ...?" I said mumbling.

"It's okay, Shelia. I mean no harm but, I have a problem."

"An elf with a problem. Well, I suppose that is natural, given that it is such a busy time of year," I said with a hint of sarcasm.

"Well, that's just it," he continued.

"What's just it?" I asked with still a hint of humour.

"The other elves and I are doing what we normally do at this time of year. It is just a week until Christmas Eve and by now, all the toys have been made but, we still have to wrap the presents, fill Santa's sack, make sure the reindeer are healthy and have plenty to eat. But this time, we have an EMERGENCY!"

"Really? What type of emergency? Do I need to call an ambulance?" Suddenly, I got a look that I never thought I would see. This time, I realised that sarcasm was not the answer.

"Well, you see, Santa Claus has disappeared!" The sad look on his little face almost broke my heart.

"Ok ... well, maybe he's just gone on a break, to take a rest before Christmas Eve," I said, hoping to show some compassion.

"No, we have been living with Santa for years and never once has he left us for this long. Even on Christmas Day, we eat dinner together as a family and he allows us to eat as much candy as we like. Elves like candy."

Buddy's mouth was now frothing as he stared at the sugar I left on the counter. "Would you like some sugar?" I asked.

Well, he jumped with delight and munched his way through the bag. He was rattling about in the bag like a hamster. Then, I could hear faint voices coming from the bedroom.

"Shelia, are you coming yet? We are cold and tired and ..." it was the boys.

"Yeah, I'm coming, just give me a minute."

I had just met an elf who was eating our sugar and he couldn't find Santa. Now, how was I supposed to explain that to my brothers? They'd think I'd gone crazy.

"No, they won't!" said the elf as he poked his little head out of the sugar bag.

"What do you mean, they won't?" I said in a rather high voice, forgetting about the boys who were waiting patiently in the bedroom.

"They won't think you've gone crazy because, I will explain to them that you are going to help me to find Santa Claus in the North Pole," said the elf. He looked pale with so much sugar stuck to his face.

"Eh! I am going to do what now?" I said a bit too loud.

"Do you always talk to yourself," said the elf and then, *poof* ... He was gone.

"Shelia, what's going on?" said Ronan, as he came barging into the kitchen.

I looked around frantically for the elf. I couldn't see him anywhere. "Eh, I burned the milk on the range so, I'll have to start again. Sorry!"

My eyes were scanning the kitchen.

"It's okay. Come on; we are waiting to hear more of your story and, it is getting really cold."

"Go on, you can have them. They're in the top drawer," I said as I was still trying to work out in my head where the elf had gone. Besides, I still don't know why my brother is so obsessed with those socks.

"Thanks Shelia, you're the best but ... are you alright? You seem, I don't know, maybe a bit out of sorts. Do you have Liam's bug?" Ronan asked me, concerned. "Only, I was full sure I could hear you talking to someone while we were in the kitchen."

"No! No! I'm fine. Just me talking to myself, thinking of more ideas to add to the story."

I couldn't tell him what I just saw, especially since I had no proof, except an empty bag of sugar. That was it. My imagination and storytelling were causing me to see things that weren't there and I was completely fine. Then, I heard laughter coming from the bedroom. And the reality hit me. The elf was in the bedroom.

"What are they laughing at?" asked Ronan, not knowing what just happened in the kitchen moments before he walked in.

"I don't know," I answered hesitantly.

"Well, whatever it is, it sounds better than your story," Ronan commented with a grin.

"Alright, do you want my socks or not?" I was on edge now about the elf.

"Ok, I'm shutting up now!"

Chapter 3

To the North Pole

Ronan and I went to the bedroom to check on the boys but, we were not prepared for what we were about to see. The elf, who I thought had been a figment of my imagination, was in the room. The window was open and the cold from outside had set in. It was like a winter wonderland only, things were getting crazier. The elf had shrunk Liam and James down to his size and they were causing mayhem. There were blankets and sheets hung up all around the room. Liam and James were wearing the same clothes as the elf and the place was covered in glitter.

"Ok Shelia, I'm sorry for calling your story boring but, don't you think you're taking it a bit too far? I mean turning the room into the North Pole?" said Ronan.

"Oh, that wasn't me, that was Buddy," I said, with a smirk on my face.

"What buddy? One of the girls from school helped you?" Ronan asked.

"No ... a different kind of buddy. Ronan meet Buddy, Santa's elf."

Ronan took one look at Buddy and that was it. He was gone out like a light and was lying on the floor of glitter.

"Oh dear!" said Buddy. "Do you have any more sugar? That will wake him up and give him loads of energy."

"No ..." I answered. "You kind of ate it all."

"Oh, sorry about that but, he will be alright once we get to the North Pole."

"North Pole!" I shouted this time.

"Yes, remember you are going to help me find Santa. I have already explained it to your brothers and they have agreed to help," said the elf with great confidence.

"Of course, they said yes. They are five and seven years old. They will believe anything." I probably said it a bit too hysterically.

"Ah, I see," said the elf with disappointment on his face. "You don't believe me."

"Look, it's not that I don't believe you. It's just, well, it sounds like a fairy tale and, you know, we are all supposed to live happily ever after."

"Ok, so you don't believe what you can't see but, am I not here asking you for help? Is it not me who turned your brothers into elves?" replied the elf with such faith and belief. I looked at him, Liam and James, now elves, and Ronan on the ground.

"OK!" I agreed. "Let's hope this fairy tale has a happy ending, or I will be put into a funny farm."

"What's that?" asked the elf.

"Oh, never mind, just me talking to myself." (This is just crazy.)

"Oh, alright, let's go," said the elf with a mission in sight.

"Before we go anywhere, what will we do about Ronan? I can't leave him here on the floor. He'll freeze to death." I can't believe I'm so concerned about Ronan.

"We will take him with us," said the elf.

"How are we going to get him to the North Pole?" I asked with curiosity.

"Well, first," he said, "you two need to become elves."

The elf sprinkled glitter over myself and Ronan and suddenly, we were the same size as Liam, James and the elf himself.

Ronan now started to come around on the floor. He was dazed and confused.

"Shelia, why am I dressed as an elf?" He asked.

"I don't know. Why don't you ask the elf standing beside you?" With that, he fainted again.

"It's okay," said Buddy. "Now we'll fly."

"Fly!" I said again, with my voice getting louder and more high pitched. (Must have something to do with the fact that I was now an elf.)

"Yes, we will fly!" said the elf.

"Ok, so, how do we fly? Since we don't have wings." (I was really trying not to be sarcastic and more caring.)

"You don't need wings to fly, Shelia. You just need a little bit of Christmas spirit," replied Buddy.

"But I don't have much of that," I said, secretly hoping I wouldn't have to go.

"Trust me, Shelia, your mother has given you and your brothers more spirit than a thousand birds migrating to their next home."

"What do you mean?" I asked suspiciously. (*What does my mother know?* I began thinking to myself.)

"Is everybody ready?" said the elf, quite cheerfully.

"I ... think so," I replied cautiously.

"Ok, now, everybody listen up. In order for us to fly, we first must hold hands. Then, I want you to close your eyes and remember your most exciting Christmas Day. Just remember how you felt, what presents you received, the big Christmas dinner you ate. Remember your parents and family. Now, open your eyes."

I almost didn't want to open them because my memories were so exciting. I was thinking about Christmas Day six years ago and Mammy allowed me to help her make the Christmas biscuits for the church hall sale. They have a bake sale every year to raise money for charity. Liam was only a baby so, Mammy needed a little helper and ... wait now! When I think about it, she called me an elf. She said it suited me, as I was born on Christmas Day. Now I was beginning to let my imagination run away with me but, I thought my mother might know something about Buddy.

"Shelia! Shelia!" James was calling me.

"Yeah! What do you want? Is Liam sick again?"

"No Shelia, open your eyes and look around," said Liam.

As I slowly opened my eyes, I couldn't believe what I was seeing in front of me. It was like a Christmas card that our la-di-da aunt sent us every year from the north of Ireland. Aunt Helen thinks she's the bee's knees because she lives in a really posh estate in Co. Down. If only her neighbours knew Her Majesty Helen when she used to live on a farm.

This place was huge. It was nothing like you would expect to see in story books or films on the telly. This sight was ... magical. The snow sparkled like glitter. There were soft white flakes falling gently on our faces. It was like being inside a snow globe. Santa's house was surprisingly small. It was made of thick oak and pine wood and sparkled all over. There was smoke coming from the chimney pot and the little windows were lit up in an orange glow. The house had a red front door with a small square window. On the front door hung a green wreath made with holly and it had a red velvet bow on it. The porch was decorated with candy canes, golden bells and holly.

A couple of yards from the house stood a very tall pine tree. It was decorated with Christmas lights, baubles, tinsel and a big golden star at the top. It was the best-looking Christmas tree I'd ever seen. In our house, the tree is usually bare by Christmas Day, as all the pine needles have fallen off. Then, every year, Mammy says, "Maybe we should get one of those artificial trees. Then we will have it every year."

But, when Christmas comes, she always just buys a real one. Daddy is tired of telling her to stop buying them so early but,

Liam and James put on their little puppy dog faces. Then, you can guess what happens. We end up with yet another stick-like tree for Christmas. I suppose, some would say it is tradition and that's exactly what it is in the O'Reilly household.

Chapter 4

Let's Save Santa!

After flying to the North Pole and standing outside in the freezing cold, might I add, we all just stood gazing at Santa's house.

"Are we going to go inside or what?" Liam asked.

"Oh sorry!" answered Buddy. "I was miles away in my thoughts about Santa's whereabouts. But first, let's head over to the factory."

"Ok!" said Liam, standing to attention like a soldier in the army. "You lead the way!"

Buddy looked at me. "I'm sorry to interrupt the crusade but, what are we going to do about Ronan?" I asked Buddy.

"We won't be able to carry him all the way, will we?"

"No, no!" replied the elf. "We will call on the troops!"

"The troops!" I said with sarcasm. For some reason, I just keep putting my foot in my mouth. "Hhm ... I mean, the troops, that sounds good."

(A little more enthusiasm, that's more like it, Shelia, I thought to myself.)

Buddy then made a strange noise with his teeth, like a squirrel trying to crack open a nut. Then, after thirty seconds, lots of little elves, possibly fifty of them, who looked just like us, came marching through the snow with a little sleigh. They each surrounded Ronan and worked together. One elf took control of the troops.

"Alright everyone. On my count. 1, 2, 3 ... lifty, upsey and downey."

Ok, since when did elves, especially these elves, use what we in Ireland call baby talk? I haven't heard words like that since Baby James was... (*Oh, hold on there now*, I muttered to myself. *Every time I learn something more about these elves, my mother is the common factor. My mother knows about this trip to the North Pole and that is why she has gone to Dublin.*)

"Are you ready, Shelia? Come on!" I could hear James calling me from my thoughts.

"Yes, James, I'm ready! Now let's go and save Santa."

Well, his little face lit up. He knew now that all the stories Mammy ever told him were true. Fantasy was now becoming reality for me too. As we slowly walked behind the elves, who were pulling Ronan on the sleigh, we held each other's hands tightly and our hearts were beating so fast, it was as if they were going to jump out from our little elf chests.

As we followed the troop of elves for about ten minutes, it became very tiring on our tiny feet. Then, suddenly, Buddy yelled out with relief, "We are here, our new friends. We are here!"

If I ever wanted to work, build or live in a factory, this was it. If Aunt Helen could see us now, she would be soooo jealous.

The closer we got to the factory, the bigger it got. The colour on the outside walls was red and silver. It looked as if Willy Wonka and the witch from Hansel and Gretel designed a factory and came up with this. I don't know much about construction but, this was first class. The building had candy canes, gingerbread men, marshmallows, toffees, fudges and little chocolate drops spewing out from the chimney pot on top of the roof. There were only two words for it, 'sugar heaven'. For the first time since we arrived here, I was actually excited, just like an elf on a sugar high. When we approached the tall archway at the door of the factory, we walked behind the elves who were pushing Ronan on the sleigh.

"I still can't believe he hasn't woken up yet," I whispered to Liam and James.

"That's because he doesn't believe, Shelia," said James.

"Believe in what?" I asked James.

"Shush! Shelia we are about to go in."

(I can't believe my two younger brothers just shushed me.)

Buddy had climbed up the big doors and rung a big golden bell, which hung down from the porch. The two doors started to open slowly and then, suddenly, everything became noisy. There were lots of elves, walking back and forth. Some were running with toys in their hands, others were... well, let's just say, it was chaos. I could never have imagined this scene to be part of my Christmas story and, now I know why. It was real.

The elves carried Ronan right down to a room near the end of a long corridor. We followed them, looking around, trying to soak up all the atmosphere. It was incredible. It definitely beat being at home in Mayo, looking out the window at the endless wind, rain and snow. Oh yeah, and the floods in spring. Some people might say that the Irish are lucky. Well, I for one don't feel that way at any time of the year.

The elves brought Ronan into a little room with a bed made of marshmallows. They laid him down gently and left the room to re-join the chaos they were are a part of. When we entered the room, there was a sign on the door that said, 'Elf Hospital' and then, of course, I thought, *Why doesn't that surprise me?*

After everything that's happened in the past four hours, anything is possible - even a hospital for elves. Ronan, of course looked very comfortable, snoring his head off. As if he didn't have a care in the world. Although, at this moment, I would have liked him to wake up. He was missing all the fun and I was missing him. Maybe it's a twin thing. I don't know, he drives me mad when we are at home.

Suddenly, there was movement. Ronan began rubbing the sleep from his eyes. I went straight over to the marshmallow bed and he looked at me in bewilderment. "Shelia" was the first word that came out of his mouth. "Is the story over yet? Only, I don't feel so good."

"No, it's not over yet; we have a few more chapters to go. Ronan, do you remember what happened before you fell asleep?" I was loving this.

"I remember going into our bedroom and the place was all draped in blankets and, frost was all over the room. Liam and James were dressed as elves and there was a friend of yours called Buddy, who helped you to make up a Christmas story you were telling the boys."

"Ok, very good, you are still with us then."

"Of course, Shelia, I haven't gone mad or anything."

"Ronan, listen to me now very carefully and please don't faint."

"Ok, why would I want to do that?" Ronan asked confused.

"Just listen, ok! About four hours ago, we were in our bedroom where I was telling you all about Santa and his elves. Well, in the meantime, a real elf came into our home and, well, he needs our help."

"Ok, ok, Shelia, do you want me to get into character for the story too? Is that it?" said Ronan, still unaware of where he was or what he was seeing.

Then, it hit me. When we came to the North Pole, James said that Ronan was asleep because he didn't believe. Now it really hit me. Ronan, like me, had no Christmas spirit. But if Mammy gave us spirit, where was Ronan's?

After trying to convince Ronan that it wasn't a Christmas story but the real deal, I gave up. I just raised my arm and showed him the whole room, as if I was the conductor of an orchestra. Ronan sat up quickly and was astonished at what he was seeing.

"Shelia, we're elves!" he shouted at the top of his new, high-pitched voice. "But I don't understand," said Ronan.

"Neither do I," I replied, "but we will soon find out."

Then, Buddy stepped in and waved at Ronan.

"Hi there, I'm Buddy, it's nice to finally meet you."

"Eh, hello, I guess, my fellow elf!"

"Ah, there you go, I told your sister you would be fine. Do you see Shelia? His sense of humour is still intact."

"Well, Buddy, humour is what you call it but, I call it annoying," I replied and stuck out my tongue at Ronan.

"Yes, that's Shelia alright. Even as an elf she can be ..."

"Stop!" Liam interrupted Ronan.

"We have been brought here to help find Santa so can we start ... please?"

"Yes, we can Liam, thanks for your reminder."

Buddy jumped in, "Are they always like this at home?"

Then, James looked at Buddy and gave him a silent approving nod of the head.

"Ok ... so where do we start?" I asked.

"It's funny you should ask that Shelia," said Buddy, "because the story regarding Santa's disappearance is a bit like you and Ronan."

"Really, how?" I asked concerned but, I was also a little bit nosy. Being Irish, it tends to come naturally.

"Well, you see, it all happened two months ago ..." Buddy began.

Chapter 5

A Grumpy Elf

"It was just another day here at the toy factory. Everyone was working hard and Santa was helping us to check how much stock we had made this year, so far. Santa and the wise old elves were deep in conversation about how Santa thought there might be a big request for mountain bikes this year. Santa's list from the previous year had a few of them and Santa thought they were becoming more popular among the children."

We all sat around Buddy, listening to every word he was saying. This sounded like a brilliant story.

"In the meantime," Buddy continued. "There was an elf called Freddy Freeze, who used to be part of our family. Freddy could be a little, well ..."

"GRUMPY!" chimed in the other elves in chorus.

"Yes, he was a little on the grumpy side. He would never talk to any of the other elves and, if they tried to be friendly towards him, he would be rude and tell them to go away. So, as I was saying, Santa thought there was going to be a big demand for mountain bikes so, he made a decision. He thought that once all of the mountain bikes were made, Freddy should be the elf to test them. You see, even though

Freddy came across as cold and rude at times, he was perfect for the job.

“Freddy Freeze, as the name suggests, was the best elf for cold weather. Even though we have all lived in the North Pole for a long time, Freddy is the only one with thick skin to endure the harshest weather. So, of course Santa naturally chose Freddy for the job but, it was a big task. It meant that every day, Freddy would have to take out the bikes to the highest snowy mountains, to test their structure and agility. Santa had made his decision but, what he didn’t know was that Freddy just happened to be listening to the conversation that Santa was having with the wise old elves. Freddy misunderstood the conversation and thought Santa was sending him to live in the snowy mountains because, he treated elves rather harshly. Freddy was offended by this but, we never thought he was going to do what he did next. Freddy went off to the mountains by himself but, not before he did the most terrible thing possible.”

“Oh no! What happened?” asked James in shock.

“Well, Freddy took something belonging to Santa that all of his elves know not to touch, let alone steal!”

Buddy used the word ‘steal’ like it was a secret but, in my house, with three brothers, stealing was common. Maybe this story did refer to me and Ronan and I was starting to connect a lot of dots. Buddy continued.

“In Santa’s house, where he and Mrs Claus live, Santa has a crystal globe of the world. Inside this globe is a clear setting of all the countries in the world. Each country has a light and when every boy and girl makes a wish for Santa to bring them a special gift for Christmas, the light remains bright and shines out across the globe. But, when the light goes out, the globe becomes dark and cold. Well, the night before Freddy took off for the mountains, he went to Santa's house. He fooled Mrs Claus by telling her that Santa had sent him to collect some of the light from the globe. You see, sometimes, when the machines in the factory become a bit strained and we like to get a certain batch of toys finished, Santa uses some power from light in the globe, just to fire up the machines so we get the work finished. So, Freddy used his opportunity to steal some of the light for himself. He took the light with him to the highest mountain in the North Pole. If the light Freddy holds in the mountain continues to shine without control, the snow could start to melt."

"If the snow melts in the North Pole, this would be a disaster for all human and animal life. The world will start to experience high sea levels and flooding. There is a reason the light must be kept in the globe. Christmas time is the time of the year when people's spirits are highest and so, the light is strongest."

"Ok, that sounds as if it would make one bestseller of a book," I commented.

One minute we were talking about Santa and the elves and now, we were on to grumpy elves stealing Christmas spirit and possibly destroying the world. All of this, well, I'm sorry but, it just sounded crazy.

"So, what happened to Santa?" asked Liam.

"Well that's where you come in," replied Buddy. "When Santa had realised what Freddy had done, he was disappointed and sad. He blamed himself for Freddy's actions and decided to go and look for him, to make amends. Santa set off on his sleigh four days ago, to find him. He took Rudolph and Prancer with him and none of them have been since. We don't know if Santa made it to the highest mountains. All we do know is that the crystal globe is losing light and, we are running out of time.

All of a sudden, Ronan stood up and lost his balance. He landed back on top of the marshmallow bed.

"Whoa! I guess I'm not used to the small elf body yet but, I could definitely get used to this bed."

For the first time in my life, I laughed with Ronan instead of at him. I didn't feel the need to criticise him or start to engage in the usual banter we get into. I think, for the first time, I have realised my twin brother is not just an annoying brother but a possible friend. Ah no! Who am I kidding? The minute we get home, we'll probably be at it like cats and dogs again. Anyway, back to Ronan.

"We have to help the elves and Mrs Claus find Santa and ... eh, where is Mrs Claus?" I asked.

"Back in the house," replied Buddy.

"Does she not come in here to the ..."

"Toy factory!" said Liam cutting me off.

"Thanks. The toy factory."

“She used to,” said Buddy. “Since Santa left to look for Freddy, she stays in the house keeping watch on the crystal globe.”

Buddy and the other elves looked very sad.

Then Ronan asked, “Can we meet her and let her know that we have come here to help you find Santa?”

“Well, of course,” said Buddy cheerfully.

“We would have brought you to meet her before but, you were asleep so, we had to bring you to the elf hospital first.”

“Oh, ok,” Ronan answered, while looking around the room. I didn’t know yet if everything had sunk in with him but, I thought we should just trust the elves now and help them for once.

“So off we go to Santa’s house,” said Buddy with excitement. “And how do you think we will get back to Santa’s house?” Buddy asked with a look in my direction.

(Now, who’s being sarcastic? I thought to myself.)

“Eh ... let’s fly!” I suggested back.

Chapter 6

Santa's House

So here we were, back at Santa's house, which we had seen when we arrived. It was an average-sized wooden house with a red door and decorated with candy canes and bells.

"Well, Santa must love Christmas with all these decorations," said Ronan.

"No, that's all Mrs Claus. She loves Christmas and we are like her children. Let's just see if she will answer the door," said Buddy with a sigh.

"Here we go!" Each of the elves, all ten of them, stood on each other's shoulders and made an elf ladder. Buddy was on top of the ladder and he reached up to pull the doorbell. After the first ring, there was no reply. Not even a creak in the small wooden house. Buddy looked down on us and his fellow elves and shrugged his shoulders. "What do we do now?" shouted Buddy from the top of the ladder. All of the elves started to natter amongst themselves with their tiny voices. Then they replied back, "Again, again!"

Ronan, Liam and James even joined in. Buddy pulled on the doorbell for the second time and then, we could hear a thump. As elves, this sounded really loud to our pointy ears and, we could hear footsteps, large ones, being shuffled across the wooden boards.

"Hello ... is there anyone there?" came an old, creaky but sweet voice from beyond the red door with a little window.

"'Tis only us, Mrs Claus, the elves from the toy factory. We have come to check on you and we would like you to meet some friends of ours," replied Buddy.

"Oh my sweet dears, come on in! Let me open the door for you. As the door slowly opened up, Buddy and the elves returned back to the ground. Each one of us peeping in through the door as Mrs Claus slowly drew it back. Then, there she was, Mrs Claus in all her radiance.

When she had completely opened the door, we realised we would never had imagined this figure in any Christmas tale. Mrs Claus was a rather small woman. Her hair was long and was as white as snow. She wore a white blouse, a red skirt just below the knees, a red apron and a pair of black boots. There was no doubt about it – she was the girl version of Santa. Well, only thinner, I suppose as Santa is supposed to be larger, well that's what we learn in books and TV. There was definitely something radiant about Mrs Claus. From the moment she looked us, you could see how warm and kind-hearted she was.

"Well, hello dears, who do we have here?" Mrs Claus put out her small frail hand to greet us.

Buddy then told her, "This is Shelia, Ronan, Liam and James O' Reilly. They have come from a small country called Ireland and they want to help us find Santa."

"Oh my!" replied Mrs Claus. "I wasn't expecting this news."

Then, Liam and James joined in. "That's right. We have decided to join the elves and go to rescue Santa from Freddy Freeze."

"Well, aren't you two very brave elves?" Mrs Claus replied with humour. "Do you need my help?" she asked Liam and James.

"No, no!" replied Liam. "You leave everything to us and Buddy. We will have Santa back before Christmas," Liam said confidently.

"I'm sure you will," Mrs Claus answered.

Then she looked at Buddy and whispered quietly to him.

"Are you sure it is safe to bring these children off out on a wild goose chase. They are human and it will exhaust them. Maybe we should wait and let Santa deal with Freddy," said Mrs Claus with concern.

"I know what you mean," replied Buddy. "But these aren't just children from another part of the world; they are some of Santa's chosen children."

"Oh!" and, with the nod of her head and a wink of an eye, Mrs Claus approved.

"Pardon me! Mrs Claus and Buddy," interrupted Ronan. "I don't suppose you know where to find and rescue Santa."

"Ah! That bit is easy," Buddy said looking at me.

Of course, we all know what that means. "We fly!"

"Well I can't let you all go off on a journey without any supplies or sense of direction," said Mrs Claus with action in her voice. "We must all put our heads together and figure out the best place to start."

"You're right!" said Buddy. "What do we do first?"

"Well, let's have a look at the crystal globe," said Mrs Claus.

"Yes, of course," replied Buddy. "Wherever Freddy is, he will be using the light to protect himself."

"Exactly!" replied Mrs Claus. Just as we all gathered around the crystal globe, there was a little voice, which came through the intense silence.

"Excuse me, hmm, excuse me!" Everyone glanced around behind them and there she stood. This tiny little elf, standing beside the red door. She was a lot smaller than the rest of us. "Holly, what are you doing here? You should be back at the toy factory where it is safe," said Buddy, very concerned for this tiny creature.

Holly was a baby elf but she looked like a ladybird on your hand. Her clothes were the same as all the other elves except that they were pink and silver in colour. She had little brown curls on her head and really bright, blue eyes. She looked like a miniature doll.

"I'm sorry, Buddy, for coming over but, there is something I think you should know."

"Ok, little one, come here to Buddy and tell me."

Buddy called the creature to him and all of a sudden, she just hovered in the air and floated over to him. I guess elves can fly at a very young age. Maybe they are even born with that skill. The little elf floated into Buddy's arms and he gave her a big hug.

"So there, little treasure, what's the news from the factory?" Buddy asked her, as if she was his little spy or reporter.

"Well," she began excitedly. "I was just floating through the factory, checking all of the toy departments to see if any of the elves needed my help. I was passing by the area where we make the mountain bikes and I noticed something strange. The tools were missing. So, then I decided to look around and check all the other bicycle sections but, all their tools were gone too. I think somebody may have taken them, so I had to come and tell you."

"Yes, you did, little one and I am so glad we have you on our team at the factory."

"And so is Santa," Mrs Claus joined in.

"Thank you very much for coming to see us Holly. You have been very helpful but now, you must return to the safety of the toy factory, or your mother will be very worried," Buddy reassured her.

"Ok, Buddy," Holly sounded sad.

"You see, I need you to go back and keep an eye on the factory because," said Buddy. "We are going on a special 'Mission'."

"A 'mission'?" Holly perked up. "What's a mission?" she asked.

"Well, a mission is like a task that we have to do when making toys. It's very important and it may take a little while for us to complete."

"Ok! So, what is the mission you have to complete?"

"Well," said Buddy. "Can you keep a secret?"

"Yeah!" Holly nodded her head up and down.

"Well, do you see these elves here?" Buddy pointed us out to her. "This is Shelia, Ronan, Liam and James. They are chosen elves that have come to help us with our mission. They have come from a small country called Ireland and they are going to help us to find Santa."

"Oh wow! That sounds great." Holly leaped with joy.

"Would you like to meet them?" Buddy asked her.

Holly nodded with a big grin on her face.

Ronan stepped forward first and introduced himself.

"Hi there, my name is Ronan," and she shook his hand. Then Liam and James came forward and shook her tiny hand. I stepped forward next and, all of a sudden, Holly just took a big leap into my arms.

"Hi!" I said after the shock I got. "My name is Shelia and you must be Holly."

"You're a girl elf just like me," she replied back and wrapped her twig like arms around me, as if I was a tree.

"I am so happy to meet you."

"I am very happy to meet you too," I said to her, whilst trying to breathe as she was clinging to me.

"Ok, ok, Holly. Let Shelia go," said Buddy.

"Oh, I'm sorry Shelia," Holly looked at me with those blue eyes that no one could say no to.

"That's alright, I'm very excited too, you know. We don't have anything like your magnificent toy factory back at home. This place is very magical."

"Yeah, it is the best!" she said.

"So, would you mind returning to the toy factory while we go on our special mission?" joined in Buddy.

"Oh, yes!" replied Holly. "Right away! Do you think I will get to see you again after your mission?" Holly asked me.

I didn't even know what was going to happen during our mission, never mind after it. I looked at Buddy for some intervention.

"Of course you will!" replied Buddy. "And, when we rescue Santa, we will come home and have a big party in the factory. Would you like that?" asked Buddy.

"Yes! Yes! Yes!" exclaimed Holly. "And I will be in charge of decorations and sweets," she said.

"I'm sure they will be the best!" I told her. Then she gave me a big hug. One of the other elves then accompanied her back to the toy factory.

"Goodbye everyone!" she said as she waved back.

"Goodbye Holly!" we all waved to her.

When the red door closed, everyone gathered back around the crystal globe, Santa's most precious possession. The crystal globe was really out of this world. It looked like New York City inside a large snow globe. The lights sparkled like stars and they shone brightly all over the world, even in Ireland. The light was captured inside the glass and when you stood close to it, it was like standing in front of a fire. If this globe was an ornament, I would definitely want one. It was mesmerising. At the bottom of the globe there was a little tap. The tap had a lever on the top that you could pull up and down. Mrs Claus and the other elves were looking all around this magical ball, trying to find anything unusual. Then Buddy saw it. It was right in the middle of the North Pole. There was a huge light, like a star, growing brighter and stronger.

"Look!" said Buddy. "That has to be Freddy. The North Pole doesn't consume that much power on its own."

"You're right!" joined in Mrs Claus. "Let's grab a magnifying glass and compass." Mrs Claus came back and stared at the globe. "Yes, I see it now. The power is travelling about twenty kilometres east of the pole."

"Well, that's not good!" one of the other elves remarked with concern.

This elf, that we got to know on our mission to rescue Santa, was called Theodore Truffle. He was a very prim and proper elf, unlike Aunt Helen. This particular elf was clearly very intelligent: he wore glasses and very smart elf attire. He had a hint of gold on his clothes and spoke with a pleasant but, rather posh accent, like I hadn't heard before.

"Why is that not so good?" enquired Buddy, with a worried look on his face.

Theodore informed us all that there happened to be a family of polar bears living in that region.

"If the power of the light becomes strong, it will melt the ice causing avalanches or flooding or..."

"Or?" again Buddy asked getting more anxious.

"Or, if Freddy decides to keep the light to himself, the North Pole and the rest of the world could become colder. Then we all might, even the polar bears, begin to freeze. Really, there is no win-win situation here," continued Theodore.

"Oh no, Shelia! Are we going to freeze like ice pops?" a frightened James asked.

"No, James, we are going to be okay and so are the polar bears. Remember, we have been chosen to come here and help the elves find Santa. Then that's what we are going to do. Right!" I glanced at Buddy.

"Right!" he replied. I also stared at Theodore.

"Well, of course we are!" replied Theodore.

"Right, so how do we go about finding Freddy and where is he hiding?" asked Ronan.

"First," said Mrs Claus "I will fill up a few small backpacks for you all, so you will have plenty to eat on your mission. Then, we will get a map from the factory and we will fill a small jar of Christmas spirit from the globe, which can be used whenever you need it."

"Now that's a plan!" said Liam.

"So ... are ... we going to fly again?" There it is; I said it – the 'fly' word again.

"Yes, we are, Shelia and, we have one more bit of info for you about our mission that you are going to love," insisted Buddy.

"Oh yeah, what's that then?" I asked cautiously.

"You're leading the mission!"

(*Help me?* I silently said to myself.)

CHAPTER 7
Learning to Fly

"Go Shelia! Go Shelia! Go Shelia!" Everyone started cheering for me, except Ronan, who was laughing at me.

"Alright, calm down everyone."

I had all these little voices in my head, cheering me on, together with fear as, I hadn't the faintest idea how I was supposed to lead a group of elves through, what only can be described as a freezer of a North Pole and, find a man who wears a red suit, has a white beard and gives presents to children all over the world on Christmas Eve.

(Are you sure this isn't just one big dream? I asked myself.)

"Ouch! Why did you do that?" I reached down to rub my leg.

"Shelia, are you away with the fairies again or something? You're supposed to be leading our mission," Ronan asked, after kicking me.

"Oh no, Ronan, the fairies don't live in the North Pole, it's too cold," Buddy answered.

"Thank you, Buddy! Now do you hear that, Ronan? Fairies don't live here so, stop interrupting me."

"Ooooh, are we finally seeing the old Shelia back again?" commented Ronan.

"Yes, you are," I said. "So, let's do this." I took control. "So has everybody got their backpack?"

"Check!" all the elves echoed back.

"Have we got the map?"

"Check!"

"Compass?"

"Check!"

"Has everyone got on your warmest clothes?"

"Check!"

"And most importantly, have we got our jar of Christmas spirit?"

"Check!"

(Good, I think we are going to need it, I muttered to myself.)

We all lined up in a row with our backpacks, all ready for the off. There were ten of us in total: Me, Ronan, Liam, James, Buddy, Theodore and four other elves named Carmel Coffee, Coco, Pudding and Sugarsnap. Mrs Claus stood in front of us and wished us all the best and a safe return home. At that moment, I remembered back to a couple of hours earlier, when I was about to tell my brothers a Christmas story I knew absolutely nothing about and, how I was really anxious and nervous awaiting the hour the boys would go to bed. Well, guess what? Here I am in the same situation. Anxious and nervous only now, I have to create some Christmas spirit so we can fly and go to rescue Santa.

"Remember, Shelia, you have loads of Christmas spirit. You just have to believe and it will guide you." Buddy gave me some advice. I mean, who can ever say in their lifetime, 'I remember one time when I got some really good advice from an elf'?

"Come on, Shelia, you can do it!" Ronan called to me from the end of my train of elves.

"Ok!" I replied with a gasp. "Here goes nothing. Everyone join hands. Now, think of the most memorable Christmas you've ever had and let your spirit guide you."

In less than two minutes, we were hovering about five feet in the air. I was, of course, lost in the memory of me and my mother making biscuits in the kitchen. The flour was everywhere – on the floor and in my hair – and Mammy was laughing hysterically.

"Shelia, Shelia!"

"Yes, Buddy, I'm here, what's wrong?"

"Open your eyes," Buddy whispered softly to me. When I opened up my eyes, I could hardly breathe. We were all flying through the frosty air, just like birds only without the wings. I looked up at the sky and it was black, full of tiny glittering stars. The ground was covered in sheets of snow and ice. I never thought I would say this but, it was the most beautiful scene I had ever witnessed. If this was a dream, as I originally thought it was, well, then I never wanted to wake up. All of the other elves and my brothers still had their eyes closed. This experience will stay with me forever.

As we flew through the air, Buddy told me that we needed to take a break shortly. Even though we flew with spirit, our bodies still required some nourishment. I agreed, so Buddy looked ahead and found an area where we could rest.

“So, how do we get everyone to land safely?” I asked Buddy.

“We will guide them down slowly,” Buddy instructed.

“Ok!” I said.

I slowly allowed by body to descend onto the snow-covered ground and everyone landed gently. The elves were the first ones to open their eyes, then Ronan, Liam and James.

“Are we there yet?” asked James excitedly.

“No, not yet” I replied. “But we need to stop for a little while, to get something to eat.”

“Oh goody!” yelled James. “I’m hungry.”

“Yeah, me too!” mumbled Ronan.

“Let’s see what Mrs Claus has packed.” I looked into the backpacks.

“Yeah, candy canes, sugar puffs, candyfloss, toffee popcorn and hot chocolate!” shouted James.

“Best snack ever!” joined in Liam.

“Buddy, if you don’t mind me asking, why do we have lots of sugary snacks?” I asked.

“Because we are elves. Elves love sugary things,” Buddy looked at me as if I was supposed to know this already, now that I was an elf.

"Well, it's just we wouldn't be used to eating high sugar foods," I said not wanting to hurt his feelings.

"Oh, it's okay here, Shelia. Because you are an elf, you can eat as much sugar as the rest of us elves and, when you return home, it will not have affected you."

"Well, there you go, Shelia, you heard the elf, dig in," Ronan spoke up. Now he was like a hamster inside a sugar bag.

We all had something to eat and drink and I decided to approach Buddy about my mother and Christmas spirit.

"So, do you think our mother will be worried about us, just like Holly's mother would have been since we are not at home?" I carefully chose my words.

"Nope!" Buddy replied like he hadn't a care in the world.

"Why do you think she wouldn't be worried?" I continued.

Buddy just looked at me with a cheeky grin, stuffed his face with toffee popcorn, took a sip of his hot chocolate and said, "So, I'm finished. Is everyone else ready to return to our mission?"

Ronan, Liam, James and all the other elves stood up quickly and answered, "Yes Buddy!"

"So, what do you say, Shelia? Should we return to our journey?" asked Buddy.

"Well, I suppose so. We need to get going before we freeze to deh ...!" James looked at me and I nearly forgot what Theodore had warned us Freddy might do. "So, we won't catch a cold," I quickly answered and his little face lit up.

(Good one, Shelia, I thought. You saved yourself there.)

"Now, my little troop, let's make sure we have all our belongings. I can't believe I'm going to say this again but, let's get back to flying."

We all placed our backpacks on our backs. Buddy rolled up the map with the compass and slid them into his belt. When we were all standing beside each other, back on our train, we held each other's hands, closed our eyes and off we went into the starry night sky. As we soared away high in the sky, it seemed a lot different to the first time we had set off. I, for some reason, felt lighter than a feather blowing in the wind. I decided to ask Buddy, "Why am I feeling so airy, like a feather this time that I'm flying?"

"Oh, that will be the sugar kick," he replied. "It will be okay. You will get used to it," Buddy said reassuringly.

Then I thought, he must be right. I've gotten on board with the rest of the craziness so, what's a bit of sugar.

As I was daydreaming, Buddy called to me with excitement, "Look! Look! Shelia, we are here. We have found Freddy and Santa."

"Well, I never!" I gasped.

This was extraordinary. I almost lost my speech. It was like looking at the mountain of dead American presidents. What's it called again? That's it – Mount Rushmore.

CHAPTER 8

A Mountain to Climb

Freddy had used the spirit from the crystal globe and used it intelligently. He had managed to create a sculpture of a huge mountain bike on top of a really high mountain. The mountain was made of ice. The work that went into carving out the mountain bike was first class. The wheels were huge and the handlebars stretched out from east to west. The saddle stretched high up into the clouds. The pedals, which had lifelike chains attached, were turning around and around. It looked like the pedals were hollow and when they reached the ground, you could jump on.

"So, now that we are here, what do we do next?" I asked Buddy.

"I don't know," replied Buddy. "You're in charge."

"I was afraid you were going to say that. I suppose, the first thing to do would be to land on the ground and figure out a plan."

"Yeah, that's a good idea," answered Buddy.

"Ok, everyone open your eyes!" I called out when we landed.

The elves, Ronan, Liam and James slowly opened their eyes.

"Where are we now?" Ronan asked.

"Look up," I replied back.

"Wow!" Everyone held their breath. "Who would have thought Freddy had such talent? He is always so rude and grumpy," Theodore remarked.

"Yes, he is but, he always makes sure that his work is perfect," said Buddy.

"Do you think Freddy and Santa are here?" asked Liam.

"Yes!" replied Buddy. "I have had a look at the map and checked the compass. The strength of the spirit is escalating."

"Well, now that we are all here, we need a plan. How do we enter this mountain bike thing? Does anyone have any ideas?" I asked because basically, even though I was the leader, I had nothing.

"Look!" said James, "look at the pedals. Maybe we could climb on and catch a ride on them, and we can get to the top."

"That's brilliant," said Buddy. "Well done James."

"Yeah, let's do that!" I agreed.

So, we all shuffled our little feet and headed towards the enormous pedals. When one of the pedals reached the ground, we all stepped on. The pedal slowly turned until, finally, we were at the top. Big mistake of course. You see, even though the big mountain bike looked like a big mountain bike, it wasn't. It was made of ice. We were like skittles that were knocked down with a bowling ball. We were all sliding up and down the bars of the bike. None of us could stop and then, a light came on. Then another and another. We decided to lie down on our bellies and grab with our nails to get some sort of grip. As we lay there, we frantically looked around for Freddy. Then we could hear a tiny voice coming from above.

"Who's there? Who dares enter my home without an invitation?"

We all looked at each other in horror, not knowing what to say. We knew it was Freddy because it had a small grumpy voice.

"Shelia!" Buddy whispered, "You say something."

(*Why me?* I thought to myself. *He's your Santa* but, I had to stop and remind myself that this was a mission and I was the leader.)

I took a big deep breath and spoke up. "'Tis I, Shelia."

"Shelia who? I don't know any Sheila in the North Pole. Where have you come from?" Freddy continued.

"I am from Ireland," I told him.

"Oh, ok, so why are you here at my home?"

"Because I want to talk to you."

"About what?" Freddy asked. "About, about..." Think, Shelia, think. "About mountain bikes!"

Buddy gestured a thumbs up at me like I was doing a good job.

"What do you want to know about mountain bikes?" he asked me, not so grumpily this time.

"Well, how to make one, of course. You see, I have three brothers who love mountain bikes and well, I would really love to know how to make them, so I could give them one as a Christmas present."

"Sure, why would you want to do that? Why can't they just ask Santa for one, like other children?" he insisted.

"That is a good idea but, you see, I am having a bit of a problem at the moment, that I would love to share with you. Perhaps inside, some place warmer." I tried to get Freddy to open up.

"No, no, you can't be bothering me now. I'm very busy so go away," Freddy shouted at me. (*Damn it, Shelia.* I reckoned I had him there.)

"Oh well, if you're busy, maybe I could help you instead." I had to wait a minute for him to answer.

"No, I don't need your help or anyone else's. Now, leave my house at once." Freddy sounded very annoyed now.

I heard him shuffle away from me, near the top of the bike. Then, the sound stopped and the shuffling came closer.

"Hey, down there." Freddy had come back. "How did you find me and what are you doing in the North Pole?"

"Those are two very good questions," I answered.

"Well, go on then; I'm waiting for an answer."

I was trying to think of an answer and then it came to me. "I am an elf who has come a long way, wanting to help a fellow elf." I thought that was a good enough answer.

"Then you lied to me," replied Freddy.

"I don't understand how I lied to you." I even had myself confused.

"You told me you wanted to know how to make a mountain bike for your brothers and now all of a sudden, you're an elf who wants to help other elves. Which answer is the truth?" Freddy sounded cross.

"Both!" I replied. "I would like to know how to make a mountain bike and, I would also like to be of assistance to you." Ok, so I know I sounded a bit desperate but, let's just see if Freddy falls for it.

"No, I don't believe you. How exactly did you get to the North Pole?" He knew something wasn't right.

"I flew ... you know ... because I'm an elf."

"But there is no elf called Shelia back at the faa ..."

He didn't finish his sentence. Something was up and Freddy knew it.

"If you fly back in a westerly direction you will find elves that you can help. Now, as I said before, I am very busy ... so goodbye!" Freddy snapped and shuffled away.

I looked at Buddy and shrugged my shoulders. I didn't know what else to do. It was also getting very cold and if we moved, we would lose our grip and slip.

"Shelia, Ssh... Shelia, I'm cold," James said, clattering his teeth.

"I know, James, it's going to be alright. We all have to pull together now and help each other to try to find Santa. Buddy, what do you think?" I was hoping Buddy would have an idea.

"Oh, that Freddy Freeze knows something!" Buddy looked at me with suspicion in his voice.

"Either he knows something or, he's just being grumpy," said Theodore.

"Ok, so let's try to find another way up to Mr Grumpy," said Ronan.

"You're right!" I agreed. "There must be another way."

Then the elf named Coco said, "Look, there are tiny little steps going along the bars of the bike and they're metal."

"Good work, Coco!" Buddy exclaimed. "Freddy obviously needed a way up to the top himself so, he created a ladder!"

"A ladder, a ladder," I repeated over and over in my head. "That's it!"

"What's it?" Ronan asked.

"A ladder. Just like back at Santa's house. Do you remember when all the elves made a ladder, when climbing up to ring the doorbell?"

"Yeah," said Ronan.

"Well, we could do it again if we all work together and pull each other up to the steps. Then we can climb up to the top where Freddy is."

"That's a really good idea Shelia," said Buddy. "Ok, so who will go first?" Buddy asked.

"Ronan!" It just came out of my mouth automatically. It's like I wanted to see him slip first, so I could laugh.

"No, no, Shelia! You're the leader so lead the way," Ronan replied with a huge smirk on his face.

"Oh fine!" I said "but, I will get you later."

"Ok, Shelia, you try to steady yourself first and then myself and Coco will follow," Buddy instructed us. "Then Theodore, Ronan, Liam, Sugarsnap, Caramel, James and Pudding."

"Hey! Why am I always the last?" whined Pudding.

"No, it's not that you're last ..." Buddy tried to say in a nice way until Theodore said, "Look Pudding, let's be realistic: you are heavier than the rest of us and we need all our strength to pull you up."

"Hey! I know that already but, it's still hurtful," Pudding replied with a sad look on his face.

Buddy tried to lighten the mood. "But you're also the best pudding maker ever!"

"Yes, I really do make some good puddings." Pudding was thrilled to be praised for his talent.

"And also the best pudding eat ..."

"That's enough, Theodore, let's get back to our ladder," Buddy interrupted Theodore from finishing his sentence. Then, Pudding stoke out his tiny tongue at Theodore.

"Looks familiar," remarked Ronan, while he glanced in my direction.

"Yes, and it is normal for us back at the factory too!" said Buddy.

"I don't know what you're talking about. Let's keep going we are wasting time," I pretended.

So, I stood up first, using my nails to grip the ice and tried to balance myself. When I managed to become still, Buddy reached for my hand and got to his feet. We continued, one by one, until Pudding was up. We held on to each other's hands tightly, so that if one slipped, we would have the strength to pull them back up. I was the closest to the iron steps so, I reached out as far as my little arms and fingers could go until I reached them. I felt like an elastic band. Then, I slowly pulled up the ladder of elves until, we were all on the steps. With me on top, we climbed the steps and kept going up and up and up. We had no way to see where we were going, as Freddy had turned off the lights and, it was like a dense fog at the top.

"Can you see anything yet, Shelia?" Buddy called out to me.

"No, the fog is very thick but, maybe we'll get there soon."

As I was climbing up the steps, I started thinking of my mother and about all the stories she told us growing up. Maybe if I had believed in them more, I might not ever have come here and ...

"OUCH!" I yelled at the top of my voice.

"Are you alright? What's happened?" asked Buddy.

"Yeah I'm okay. I just banged my head off a metal lock. Well that's what it felt like," I answered back, rather annoyed. Maybe Freddy Freeze was rubbing off on me.

"No, you're right, I can see it from here. There's a lock on the front of a small door," said Buddy.

"That must be the way in or up!" Ronan said "but, if there's a lock, that means I can't open it."

"Oh, yes you can!" replied Sugarsnap. She rooted around underneath her elf hat and pulled out a little hair clip. "Do you know how to work a lock with a clip?" she asked.

"No, not really," I replied.

"It's ok, Shelia, I will tell you what to do," said Buddy. Sugarsnap passed up the hairclip and here, I was about to learn another new elf skill.

"Ok, it's really rather easy." Buddy began with his instructions. "First, you must part the clip until it is straight."

"Ok, done," I answered.

"Then, slowly put the clip into the keyhole."

"Ok, done," I said as I was shivering and my fingers had gone numb.

"Then, just gently wiggle the clip inside the keyhole until you hear it release back. Be careful not to break the clip."

"Ok, no pressure then?" I called back.

"You are doing a really good job Shelia. It takes some of us elves a couple of hours to master this task."

"Only a couple of hours!" I replied, in my usual Shelia style.

"Oh, not I," butted in Theodore with his rather snooty tone. "I completed that task in 2.3 seconds."

"And that's brilliant," said Buddy "but now it's Shelia's turn."

"Hey Shelia, I know you are under a bit of pressure up there but, just one observation – doesn't Theodore remind you of Aunt Helen?" asked Ronan.

"Aye!" I answered Ronan with my best Northern Ireland accent. I could hear my brothers laughing.

"Well, I'm glad someone's having fun. My fingers are like a box of fish fingers that Mammy has left in the freezer for a year."

I could hear more giggling from the boys then, 'click' – I did it. The lock opened after about five minutes of wiggling.

"Well done! Yeah Shelia! Who-hoo!" everyone started to cheer.

"Thank you, thank you very much," I replied with such delight. Then ... busted!

CHAPTER 9

Freddy Freeze

How stupid were we that we hadn't noticed we were making a lot of noise on the steps? Freddy had already heard us when we were down below so, of course, he was going to hear us now that we were at his front door.

"Well, well, who do we have here?" Freddy said wickedly.

"Grumpy ... I mean, Freddy ..."

I had forgotten his name because everyone kept saying how grumpy he is and now that he caught us, he even looked grumpy. Freddy was the same size as the other elves. He wore green, red and white clothes with a silver shimmer to them. He had dark, beady eyes and red, rosy cheeks. He also had a grey beard that was sticking out like an icicle.

"Did I not make myself clear, when I told you to go away?" Freddy shouted at me. He was very angry.

"Well you did, but ..." I tried to defend myself.

"But nothing!" Freddy cut me off from offering my explanation. It's not like I had one.

"Don't you understand a simple command from an elf?"

"Well, I would only ..."

“Hi Freddy!” Buddy cut me off.

(I don’t see why I’m here at all if they don’t want me to talk, I thought to myself.)

“Who’s down there? I thought you were on your own.” Freddy peeped down the steps.

“Well, I was, you see and ...”

“It’s only me Freddy,” Buddy cut in again. Seriously why am I here again?

“What are you doing here?” Freddy finally asked Buddy, instead of me.

“Well, you see ... we were kind of out looking for Santa!”

“Oh, that old fool. What would make you think that he is here?” Freddy pretended that he knew nothing about Santa’s disappearance.

“Well, you see, when you left the toy factory, Santa went out to look for you. He hasn’t returned.”

Buddy chose his words carefully. The last thing we needed was an accused, angry and grumpy elf.

“Oh, so you all thought you could just come to my home, make a lot of noise and assume I will just give Santa back. Or, I mean, send Santa back. Or, I mean ... just go away. I don’t need any elves so, go home!” said Freddy.

“Look Freddy, it’s okay!”

“No, it’s not! Give us Santa back, now!” shouted James.

"Hey, who said that?" Freddy could now see us all on the steps.

"Hi Freddy! Hey how do you do?" all the elves called back.

"Well, if it isn't the cavalry and the chubby one."

"Hey, that's mean!" Pudding whined.

"Oh, I'm sorry, the chubby one has feelings. You're not the only one, you know."

Freddy gave me a cold stare. I felt really embarrassed. He was also hurt by everyone, back at the toy factory, calling him grumpy.

"Freddy, if it's okay with you, do you think we could come up off the steps only, it's really cold down here?" I tried asking nicely. I was cold and my teeth were chattering as if I was doing a flamenco dance.

"No, you can't!" he replied rather sharply. "I told you, I am very busy with Santa so, go away!"

"Please, Freddy, you don't want to see your fellow elves out in the cold, do you?" I thought, maybe I could gain some sympathy for the elves that he knew.

"Well, they never cared about me so, why should I care about them? You've only come here to get Santa, so he will deliver your precious Christmas presents," he replied sharply.

"I wouldn't call Ronan's presents precious. Shelia is getting him pink woolly socks," James told Freddy.

"Thanks for that James. You have ruined the surprise!" I responded. I was rather annoyed.

"Ah Shelia, come on, you could at least have chosen a different colour," Ronan joined in.

"How about red because that's what I'm seeing now," I replied frustrated.

Here we all were in the cold, on a mountain bike, fighting about what colour socks I should get Ronan for Christmas. I mean, seriously, bigger picture and all that.

"Stop everyone. We have all come here to help find Santa and, all we can do is argue. Maybe we should be thinking about why Freddy is here and not back at the factory with his own family," I snapped. It must be all the sugar: I've burned and crashed.

"Well said, Shelia. We are here to save Santa and get Christmas back the way it should be," Buddy sided with me.

"Well, this is all very touching but, this year is going to be different," Freddy announced with a menacing look.

"It doesn't have to be, Freddy. Why don't you just let us all up. You can let Santa go and we will all have a cup of hot chocolate and talk it over?" Buddy tried his best to get Freddy to let us in.

"Oh yeah, sure and, I won't be grumpy anymore," Freddy answered sarcastically. It seemed that me and Freddy may have a lot more in common than I thought.

"Yeah, you're right, Freddy. Maybe we should just leave you alone."

"Shelia, what are you doing?" Ronan interrupted.

"Shush Ronan! I'm trying to get on Freddy's grumpy side."

"But before we leave," I continued, speaking to Freddy, "we will have to help you out, like I said earlier." I had a plan.

"Yeah ... we will have to help you make this mountain bike sculpture perfect."

"What are you talking about? My workmanship skills are one hundred per cent perfect. You could not improve it in any way." Freddy was annoyed at my accusations. He had taken the bait so, now I just had to reel him in.

"Are you sure about that? Sure, we nearly broke our necks getting up here on the icy bars and, don't get me started on the poor lighting." I kept on winding him up, like a clockwork mouse.

"Rubbish!" he shouted at me. Then he started thinking about what I had said and, bingo! "Alright, up you come. The whole lot of you, move it, move it, and move it," Freddy sounded like a drill sergeant in the army.

When he let us up through the little latch door, we saw yet another magnificent creation. There was no doubt about this elf's talent. Freddy had made himself a quiet little cosy home inside a well sculpted saddle. There were little lights up along the ice ceiling and along the corridor. Well, it looked long to us because, we were elves now. The walls of the corridor were all shiny and glittery.

"You will have to put these on before you walk." Freddy gave us a pair of boots with grips on the bottom. "Well, I don't want you to fall on my creation, do I? I am a perfectionist and besides, if you get hurt, then I will never get rid of you," said Freddy.

"So, do you think we could have a look around inside your cool mountain bike?" Buddy asked politely.

"Oh, well, I suppose but, just a quick look, mind you. You are not going to steal my ideas and take them back to the factory, are you?" Freddy looked at Buddy with suspicion.

"Oh no, Freddy! I don't think anyone could recreate this. I mean, it is just out of this world."

"I could do it with my eyes ..."

"That's enough, Theodore. Remember how brilliant Freddy is at sculpting." Buddy cut in, thankfully, before Theodore made it worse.

"I was just telling the truth," Theodore answered back. "And that's always good but, let's go with Freddy and check out his creation. OK?"

"Well, seeing as we are here, it is only polite, I suppose," Theodore agreed.

We all put the boots on while Freddy stood watching us, with his hands behind his back. As we walked along the corridor, there were lots of rooms to the left and right. Each room had one door and a sheet of glass at the top half of the doors. They were all carved out of ice.

"Wow, there are loads of rooms. What are they for?" Buddy asked the grumpy elf nicely.

"It's none of your business," replied Freddy sharply.

"I'm sorry, I was just interested," Buddy said apologetically. If there's one thing that I noticed most about Buddy since we met, it's that he likes to be everyone's friend. As we continued to walk to the end of the corridor, there was a stairway that went up even higher.

"What's up there?" asked James.

"That's where I am going to make ..." Freddy stopped walking and talking and turned around.

"Hey, what's with all the questions?"

"No questions. We just want to know where Santa, Rudolph and Prancer are," said James.

"Oh, that's why you're here. You're not here to help me ... an elf." Once again Freddy looked at me.

"No, no! We are here to help. Excuse my brother, James, he is just excited. This is all new to me and my brothers and, we can't wait to get started in our new roles as elves.

"Well, that is what we will do." Freddy instructed us. "Follow me into this room and all will be revealed."

This is it. The moment we had all been freezing in the cold for. We were going to save Santa and go home but, nothing is ever as easy as it seems. When we entered the room, it looked rather ordinary. The only things that Freddy had here were the mountain bike tools.

"Are these the tools you stole from the toy factory?" James asked, shaking his head with disappointment. "Santa is not going to like that," James remarked.

"I didn't steal anything. These tools are mine and they always were. Santa borrowed them from me and I have brought them to my factory."

"What factory?" once again James talked back. I wanted to zip his mouth shut. We didn't need to make Freddy angrier than he already was.

"Yeah, that's right, you've all heard it. This is my factory and guess what I have?" We all stood there with our hearts in our mouths, trying to figure out what Freddy meant.

"Well, let me enlighten you all. First, I got myself some Christmas spirit. Second, I built myself a factory. Third, I got myself a Santa. Fourth, I got myself two reindeer and a sleigh. That was a bonus and now, fifth, I got myself ... what do you call them? Let me see. What's that word?"

I began to look around at everyone and we all had shocked faces. "Elves!" I replied.

"Yeah, that's the word, elves. All ten of them. Already, helpful and asking loads of questions because they love to learn. Well, don't just stand there with your mouths open, follow me. Hup, two, three, and four. All together now," Freddy chanted.

"Hup, two, three, four." We all had to join in.

Freddy brought us back to the stairway that was reaching high up into the air an, we couldn't see any end to it. There was a lot of cold misty fog, like a thick rain cloud only, this one was not opening up any time soon. It felt as if we had been walking for hours. It was probably only a few minutes but, if felt longer because, we had to carry the tools and we were already exhausted. Buddy looked at me and I glanced at him. Ronan looked over his shoulder at me too. I knew it was a signal – signal for me to get us out of here. I slowly managed to shuffle over to Buddy without Freddy noticing.

"Do you have any ideas of how to get us out of here?" Buddy whispered to me.

"No, I was kind of hoping you would," I whispered back.

"I think I have one," said Ronan.

I looked around at Liam, James, Caramel, Coco, Sugarsnap, Pudding and Theodore. They were all cold, hungry, tired and miserable. This is not what Santa and the North Pole are supposed to look like.

"Ronan, what's the plan?" I whispered.

"I think we might need more troops. I mean it sounds like Freddy is operating here on his own. Surely if we had more elves to help, we could fight back!" Ronan was all riled up.

"Oh, I don't like fighting," whispered Buddy, "but, your idea is not without merit."

"Do you think there is a way of contacting the elves back at the factory?" I asked Buddy.

"Yes but, it requires Santa's help."

"Oh right." Think Shelia, think. There must be another way or someone! "That's it: Holly!" I said to Buddy.

"What about her?" Buddy replied.

"Do you think there is any chance that she may have followed us? She seemed very excited about our mission when we told her."

"I suppose there is a small chance but, can we wait until then." Buddy looked at me disappointedly. "She's so small that even if she did follow us, she wouldn't be able to bear the cold."

"That's true. Santa will just have to help us, if we ever reach the top."

"We don't have to wait, you know," Theodore whispered from behind.

"We don't?" we all chimed together. We all started to listen. Theodore had a voice with authority that made you want to listen.

"No, we don't," said Theodore smugly.

"What do we have to do?" I asked.

"All we need is the map and the jar of spirit. When we get to the top, I will make a paper aeroplane from the map and add a touch of the spirit to it. I will then throw it up into the sky and, it will find its way back to the factory. Then the elves will know where we are and come to help us."

"That's genius! Why didn't I think of that?" exclaimed Buddy.

"Because I'm the intelligent one," Theodore reminded him.

"Yes, you are and now, thanks to you, we can contact the recruits."

Everyone looked up and held their heads high. We had forgotten about the cold and hunger. Now it was time for battle. Operation Save Santa.

After about twenty minutes of walking up the stairs, we finally came through the big cloud. All we could hear was a gasp. I don't know if it was a relief from walking or because of what we saw. Maybe both. At the top of this mystery stairs was a glass dome, similar to Santa's one back at the house. This glass dome was huge and it was blue in colour. You could not see inside, as it had a strong light and, I could only assume that it was where Freddy was storing the Christmas spirit he had stolen from Santa's house. Around the glass dome, there was only one entrance up to the glass door. On the outside, there were metal plates and bars all placed around but nothing had been finished. Freddy looked at us all as we stood, gazing up at the dome, almost as if in a trance.

"Hmm, I want helpful elves, not daydreamers. So, as you can see, I have yet to complete the fencing around my glass dome and, that's where you come in. Now, you've got your tools so, hop to it." Freddy ordered us around.

"Sure, no problem. Leave it to us, Freddy," Buddy answered him.

"Ok, that's good, I will just be downstairs in the factory so, don't touch the dome and, don't disturb me." Freddy marched off.

"Yes Freddy!" we all answered.

We couldn't wait for him to leave so that Theodore could put his plan into action.

"Everyone look around to see which direction is the best way we can get this map out of here," said Theodore.

We all looked around frantically, like owls, only without the hoots.

"Look over there!" cried Liam.

"What's that?"

"I don't know," replied Theodore.

"It looks like ... yes, it is ... it's a star. There is no top on the dome. I can see the stars."

"Good job, Liam," I told him.

"Yes, well spotted," Theodore remarked.

"Have you got the map ready?" Buddy asked Theodore.

"I have completed the perfect aeroplane, ready for departure. All we need is to sprinkle the aeroplane and, wallah!" exclaimed Theodore with pride.

"I have the jar here in my bag. Let me get it out," said Buddy.

"Ho, ho, cc! How, cc!"

Buddy suddenly stopped ruffling in his backpack.

"What was that sound?" Buddy asked, with his ears perked up like a dog after hearing a strange sound.

"What sound? I didn't hear anything," Ronan answered.

"Oh no! Maybe it's Freddy coming back to check on us," said James fearfully.

"It's okay, James. We are not going to let anything bad happen. Remember, we're going to get Santa back." I tried to reassure James, who was getting upset.

"Ho, ho, I!"

"Did you hear it now?" Buddy asked again.

"Yeah, I did. Where is it coming from?" I asked. We all listened now with our ears pointed high.

"Ho-ho. I'm here!"

"It's Santa!" James exclaimed with excitement.

"It's Santa alright but, where is he?" Buddy was wondering.

"In there! In there!" shouted Liam. "He's inside the glass dome."

"Well, obviously that's why we are not permitted to enter," Theodore joined in.

Suddenly, there was a big celebration going on around me. Caramel, Coco, Sugarsnap and Pudding all started skipping around and cheering.

"Santa's here! Santa's here! Let's all cheer. Santa's here!"

Liam and James, of course, joined in. Whilst they were all delighted with finding Santa, they had forgotten one thing. There was no place for us to move. We were all standing at the top of the stairs where Freddy had left us. So, what do you think happened? We all lost our balance and fell down, one after the other.

"Hold on to anything you can get a grip of," I cried out.

"Shelia! Shelia! Help!"

I looked around and he wasn't there. Where was Baby James?

Chapter 10

We Need a Plan

My heart had sunk from the North Pole to the South Pole in a split second. James was gone.

"Is everyone okay?" Buddy called out.

"Ronan?"

"Yeah!"

"Liam?"

"Here!"

"Theodore?"

"Here!"

"Caramel?"

"Yes Buddy!"

"Sugarsnap?"

"I'm okay!"

"Coco?"

"Here, Buddy!"

"Pudding?"

"Yeah!"

"Shelia?" I couldn't respond. The last word I heard in my mind was 'help'.

"Shelia, are you okay? What's wrong?" Buddy shouted, this time with panic.

The tears started to well up in my eyes.

"James is gone!" That was all I could manage to say without bursting into hysterics.

"What? Where is he?" Ronan then began to panic as well. I pointed back down the stairs. "No, no, he can't, we have to go and get him!" Ronan started to get hysterical.

"Where is James?" Liam then asked me.

"I think he fell down the stairs," I answered.

"Well, go get him!" Liam now screamed at the top of his voice. We were all terrified.

"But what if he is?" I couldn't finish my sentence.

Ronan cut in, "He's going to be fine. We're elves now; aren't we Buddy? So, he's okay, right?"

"Ronan is correct. We are an elite group," Theodore agreed.

"I can't, Ronan. What if?" I couldn't finish my sentence again because, every time I spoke, I felt my heart was going to jump out of my mouth. The tears were now streaming down my cold face like a waterfall and I was shaking like a leaf.

"Yes, you can, Shelia. Forget about everything that has happened here tonight. Forget about all our arguments. Forget about Christmas stories and forget about the pink, woolly socks. That's our brother down there and if anyone can save him, it's you. We trust you, Shelia. That's why you were chosen to lead this mission, just like we were chosen to help save Santa," Ronan said determined.

"As touching as all of this may be, could someone tell me who we are saving first? James or Santa?" said Theodore being practical.

"Theodore, you're my brother and I love you but, will you just shut up for a minute!" Pudding shouted out.

"You're brothers!" Ronan and I exclaimed in shock.

"Yeah, I'm surprised you couldn't tell," replied Pudding. "Theodore and I can't get along sometimes too but, we still love each other because, we are family."

"You speak for yourself," Theodore answered back. Pudding gave him another 'shut your mouth' look.

"James is your family. We know where Santa is now and we are not going anywhere, anytime soon. So, go and get James. He's our family too now and, Theodore can send for the troops."

"Thank you, Pudding and Ronan. I needed to hear that and you are all right. I'm going to find James!" I said confidently.

I wiped the tears from my eyes. I gave Ronan, Liam and the elves a big hug then, I slowly descended back down the stairs, taking great care going back down the steps one at a time, hoping Freddy wasn't going to catch me or frighten the life out of me. That would have been the last thing I needed. It was still very cold on the stairs and, it was exhausting work with such tiny legs and feet. (I kept thinking in my mind, *James will be okay. He's tough and, when the other elves arrive, we will be ready for action.*)

With all the other elves up above, I started to feel lonely so, I started thinking of my mother again. I know she had something to do with this trip. I must have been daydreaming for quite a while because, somewhere in the back of mind, I could hear someone singing, "You better watch out. You better not cry. You better not pout, I'm telling you why. Santa Claus is coming to town." Then it got louder. "He's making a list and checking it twice. He's going to find out who's naughty or nice."

All of a sudden, this little breeze went up my back. I looked up and I thought I was going to fall over. It was James. Thank heavens, he's alive.

"James!" I called out to him but his eyes were closed. I didn't know what was going on. There he was, my little brother, floating back up the stairway singing *Santa Claus is coming to Town*. I started to quickly climb back up the stairs behind him, forgetting about how I could easily slip at any moment. All I wanted right now was to have Baby James back in my arms. I raced as fast as I could until I reached the top. I was out of breath and panting. The other elves were still standing where I had left them. When they saw me without James, all sweating and panting, they looked like they had seen a ghost.

"What is it, Shelia? What happened? Where is James?" Ronan asked me. All I could do, until I got my breath back, was to point up. There was James floating higher and higher up. He was nearly above the glass dome that had been making Santa Claus sounds before I left. When I finally stopped panting, I asked Buddy, "What should we do? How do we get him back down?"

Buddy started to laugh.

"I don't think now is the time for humour; do you?" I was getting worried now. What if all that sugar and drama had made Buddy go crazy.

"Oh, I'm sorry Shelia. I don't mean to sound rude but, can't you see?" Buddy asked me.

"See what?" I was frantic now.

"James remembered his Christmas spirit, which, therefore?"

"... Made him fly," I continued.

"James is in no danger. When his memory returns, he will land safely. What was he doing when you found him?" Buddy asked.

"I was only halfway down the stairs when I heard his voice. He was singing *Santa Claus is Coming to Town.*

"Oh, I love that song," Buddy said cheerfully and then, all the elves started the celebration again.

"Hold it, hold it, everyone. Do you remember what happened the last time you were all celebrating?"

They all froze and looked at each other.

"We're sorry!" They all lowered their heads.

"It's okay, everyone. Now we have James back and we know where Santa is. Let's get back to our rescue mission," Buddy announced with ease.

"I'm sorry for asking, Buddy but, just how long will it be before James comes down?" I had to ask because, I wasn't able to settle my nerves until I had him back in my arms.

"Well, he is singing so, I assume, when the song has finished."

"Thanks Buddy, that's a load off my mind. So, back to our mission. What do we do about Santa?" I let out a sigh of relief.

"Well, while you were gone, myself and the other elves had a look around and, it seems the only way we can get to Santa is if we complete the surrounding platform," Buddy answered.

"But what about the troops? Did Theodore manage to send the map?"

"Why of course I did, what do you take me for?" Theodore answered, annoyed that I was questioning his ability.

"Oh, I'm sorry! I wasn't implying that you couldn't complete your task. In fact, if we didn't have you on this mission, we would probably be lost."

"Or dead!" added Ronan.

"Ok, Ronan thanks for your input. What I was trying to say before Ronan butted in was that, your intelligence is much appreciated."

"Well, thank you for noticing. There was no way I could let you rescue Santa without me."

“So, enough with the all the mushy stuff and let’s get to work,” Ronan interrupted.

Ronan always liked work. “Anything to get him out of the house,” Mammy would always say.

“Seeing as this is your first elf job, we will start you off lightly,” Buddy told us but, Ronan was having none of it.

“No light work for me, Buddy. I am a big man. I can handle it,” Ronan spoke all brave-like.

“Ok, it seems Freddy has all the right tools and supplies but first, we need a plan. Theodore!” Buddy said, knowing Theodore always has a plan.

CHAPTER 11

The Story of Christmas

Theodore, Caramel, Sugarsnap, Pudding, Coco and Buddy were amazing to watch. They were like miniature robots from the future. Theodore first drew up the plan, using a sheet of ice. He sculpted down every last detail with such precision and dedication. Sugarsnap and Caramel used a rope to connect a kind of conveyer belt, to move the iron grates from one end to the other. Buddy and Pudding then hammered and sawed away.

They divided each of us between them. Liam helped Theodore with the map because, as Theodore had commented earlier, he had very good eyesight. Liam was making observations and reporting to Theodore. I was helping Sugarsnap and Caramel. The three girls together, we made a good team. Ronan helped Buddy, Pudding and Coco with the construction. He was as happy as a pig in muck. With all the banging of hammers, pulling of robes and everyone chatting, this was like a real factory – one that Grumpy Freddy created.

As for James, well, he was still hovering in the air and had moved on to a version of *Jingle Bells*. Now, all we had to do was wait for backup. The work was coming on 'splendidly', as Theodore would say. All of the iron grates were nearly set in place. Ronan, Buddy, Pudding and Coco were doing a great job.

“I hope we get the platform finished before the troops arrive, or we will have no way to rescue Santa,” Buddy voiced his concern.

“Have there been any more sounds or movement from the dome since we first heard them?” I asked.

“No,” replied Buddy rather sadly. “I just hope we are not too late.”

“Too late for what?” Ronan asked as he managed to lift his head away from his work for a minute. “Maybe, we should continue to work and just hope for the best.”

“You may as well inform them about what might happen if our mission is a failure,” Theodore whispered to Buddy.

“But I don’t want to scare them,” Buddy whispered back.

“You want to be their best friend you mean. I will then,” said Theodore.

Theodore looked up at the glass dome and started to speak like a History teacher. Ronan was going to love this.

“Centuries ago, back in the Dark Ages, Christmas spirit was near to almost non-existent. None of the humans on Earth ever had any sense of hope, belief or faith. They would commence each day and go to the fields to work. At the end of their working day, they would return home to eat and sleep.”

“I don’t think they need the full version,” Buddy interrupted.

"No, it's good, we can listen while we work," I said to Buddy.

"Ok but, just try not to fall asleep," Buddy whispered back.

We each had a giggle under our breath.

"I heard that, Buddy but, I shall continue," Theodore composed himself.

"Like I was saying, life was without light in the olden days. That, of course, all changed with Christmas spirit. There was a special boy who was born on a very cold night, in a place called Bethlehem. With this child's birth came great faith, power, belief and magic. Call it whatever you like, it was there. It existed. As the child grew up, he gave his people something more than just a toy under the Christmas tree. He gave them life with light. His name was ..."

"Jesus!" Liam exclaimed.

"Yes, his name was Jesus and, if he had not given people life, well then, Santa and ourselves would not exist. It is with his extraordinary birth and powerful gift that the people on Earth can see and feel the light. Santa Claus' original name, St. Nicholas, was chosen by Jesus. His job was to keep the light going through the giving and receiving of gifts on Christmas Day. Over the years, Santa has managed to keep the spirit of Christmas bright."

"So, what has the spirit of Christmas got to do with Santa being inside a glass dome?" Ronan jumped in of course. That lad had no patience.

"It has a lot to do with Santa. You have all seen the crystal globe back at Santa's house. Well, Santa decided that the only way he could keep this powerful spirit in existence was to contain it in a crystal globe. The glass traps the light inside and therefore, it shines all over the world. It surrounds all people and their homelands. Anytime Christmas spirit goes low, the light may weaken but, surrounding countries empower it."

"Wow!" Liam gasped. "Is that why Santa is in that glass dome?" asked Liam.

"That's exactly why he's in there. Freddy has trapped him in there to strengthen the light that he had stolen and to keep it shining with Santa's Christmas spirit," Theodore finished.

"So, Santa is ok? He is just waiting to be rescued?" Liam asked.

"Well, we hope so but, with the sounds he was making earlier, it means he is getting physically weak."

"And what about Rudolph and Prancer?" Liam asked, concerned.

"I would like to think Freddy has them at another part of this freezer. Besides, the reindeer are no of use to him when it comes to power. They are just regular animals that need food and shelter. It is Santa's spirit that allows them to fly."

"That's a good thing, right. They're not in any danger?" Liam asked.

"No, they have a better chance than Santa does," Theodore replied forgetting once again that Liam is only seven.

It made me feel relieved that James was still flying and singing Christmas songs. At least he was away from all the drama.

Bang! Bang! Bang! "There you go, Buddy, that one is complete," Ronan said with triumph. "I'm getting good at this elf thing!" he said delighted with himself.

"You are definitely a good worker. That hasn't gone unnoticed." Buddy gave him a slap on the back.

(Buddy better be careful: all that complimenting might give Ronan a big head, I thought to myself.)

"I'm totally exhausted. Maybe we could take a break?" I looked at Buddy.

"Yeah," Buddy agreed. "What do you say, Theodore?"

"Sounds splendid. I'm rather parched myself," Theodore replied.

Then we all spread out and watched James give us a version of *Away in a Manger*. I had to admit that he had a pretty good voice for a five-year-old elf.

We gathered around and enjoyed what we had left in our backpacks. We sat on the iron grates, munching and sipping and snorting. Probably not a pretty sight but, who cared? We were starving.

"Freddy hasn't checked up on us yet and the troops haven't arrived. What do you suppose will happen next?" I asked the other elves.

"Freddy is a perfectionist, like myself. He knows exactly how long it will take to complete the platform so, it probably will be another hour or so," Theodore answered.

"Another hour but, we ... I mean ... another hour it is then." I didn't want to seem selfish but, I was. We must have been in the North Pole for hours and, all I wanted was the comfort of my own bed.

"Do you think Santa will be okay?" I looked at Buddy.

"Don't worry about Santa. He is as tough as his own boots," Buddy replied cheerfully. "How about we get back to work? If we get finished soon, we might save Santa ourselves. We all stood up, brushed off the crumbs and replied, "Yes Buddy!"

There were only two more iron grates and railings left to put in. Freddy had already completed the bridge that led to the glass dome. All we needed to do now was to complete the entrance. So, off we went back to work. Clink! Bang! Pull! After about ten minutes into our work, James stopped singing. We all looked up and he was drifting down slowly, like a feather.

"Oh look. James's Karaoke Hour must be over," Ronan announced.

James gently landed on his feet and started to rub his eyes. I ran over to him, picked him up and squeezed him like a sponge.

"Shelia, hey, I can't breathe," James couldn't move because, I was holding him so tightly.

“Oh, I’m sorry, James! Do you remember what happened?” I asked panicking, hoping he didn’t get a bang on the head when he fell down. I don’t want to have that image or memory ever again in my head. That was one experience of the North Pole I wish to forget.

“Well, I remember dancing and then I slipped but, that’s it,” James replied.

“But you’re here now and you’re all ...” I wanted to say in one piece but, I didn’t want him thinking he was like Humpty Dumpty. “I’m just happy you’re back with us because you’ve got a lot of work to catch up on.” I didn’t feel sad anymore.

“Awe! Did I miss all the fun?” James was disappointed. “What about Santa? We found him! Where is he?” James was getting excited again.

“Oh well, we have found him but, we have to complete the platform around the big glass dome or, we can’t reach him,” I explained to James.

“Aw, I wanted to meet Santa and tell him all about our mission.”

“And you will, James. Once our work is complete and when the troops arrive, Santa will be all yours,” Buddy explained and James jumped for joy.

“So, what will I do Buddy?” James asked excitedly.

“You can help me, Ronan, Pudding and Coco.”

James caught a glance of Ronan and ran to him. “Ronan, I’m going to work with you.”

It was as if James had forgotten us since his little trip.

"Hey little man, it's good to have you on our team!"

"Thanks Ronan and where is Liam?" James asked.

"Liam is helping Theodore draw up plans for the platform."

"Cool!" James was enjoying every minute.

"Well everyone, let's get back to work," Buddy said.

Now that our team was united, all we needed was the troops.

We worked harder than ever now, as we just wanted to get finished. The platforms and railings were complete and we all worked together at completing the entrance. It was becoming rather difficult. Freddy had made the bridge from a sheet of ice but, the frost kept sticking to it, which made it impossible for us to join the bridge to the iron platform.

"Theodore, do you have any idea how to attach the plates to the bridge?" Buddy asked with a serious face. If there was one thing I've learned about elves it is, no matter who had the idea, the job must be done. "This is rather a tough dilemma," Buddy said, while scratching his head.

"What if we used toffee?" shouted Caramel.

"No! Sugar," Sugarsnap shouted too.

"Hold on, you didn't let me finish," Theodore answered back, as if they had been rude to interrupt.

"Sorry," Caramel and Sugarsnap apologised while looking down and playing with the bells on the top of their boots.

"It's alright but, your ideas are not bad. We could spread sugar on the ice and make a sand like surface. That might give it some grip for us to walk. Then, maybe we could melt some toffee and use it as a filler. We could make a small stairway at the edge of the bridge."

"That's a good idea but, do you think it will hold?" Buddy asked concerned.

"Hey!" Caramel interrupted. "The way me and Sugarsnap make toffee, nothing will break it!"

"It might hold for two hours." Theodore, of course, was being realistic.

"Well that should be enough time to rescue Santa and get out of this place before we all free..." Just before Buddy could finish talking, we all stopped and heard singing.

"We all know what we've been told!"
Response: "We all know what we've been told."
"Elves are getting really cold!"
Response: "Elves are getting really cold."
"Now let's go and join the quest!"
Response: "Now let's go and join the quest."
"Santa's army is the best!"
Response: "Santa's army is the best."

"What was that?" I asked Buddy.

Buddy's eyes lit up. Sugarsnap, Caramel, Pudding and Coco started to dance. Theodore threw his eyes up to Heaven. "Do they really need that silly song?"

"Why is no one answering my question?" I asked Buddy.

"The troops have arrived," replied Buddy with relief.

Chapter 12

This Means War!

It was just as Buddy had said: The troops had arrived and now, Freddy was in for an even bigger battle. While we were all up at the top of the mountain bike, the elves had arrived and were somewhere below. We didn't know if Freddy had heard them but, judging from our arrival, I assumed he had.

"How will they know where we are?" I asked Buddy.

"Freddy will bring them in. Trust me."

Buddy gave a secret wink to the other elves. They knew what was going to happen but, I didn't. The curiosity was killing me more than the hunger and cold put together.

"Buddy?" I whispered. "What's going to happen now?" I started getting anxious.

"It's okay, Shelia. We are going to rescue Santa and the troops will keep Freddy busy."

"Do you think the sugar and toffee have set?" asked Sugarsnap

"Well, the sooner we get Santa out of here ..." Buddy began to say.

"Then, the sooner we get to take Freddy out," Ronan finished.

I know Ronan can be a bit of an idiot sometimes (well, all the time really) but, this time I could see in Buddy's eyes that he was scared. This small elf, who had appeared in my house a couple of hours ago, all high with Christmas spirit and sugar was actually scared.

"Let me check the toffee!" declared Caramel. "The steps are as solid as rocks and the sugar has stuck to the ice. I'm not sure how long it will last or how much weight it will hold?" Caramel said to Buddy.

"Well, now that the elves are here, it is time for Shelia and me to lead the rescue. We will go over the bridge and enter the glass dome to find Santa. Theodore will take charge out here. You must watch out for Freddy and the troops. We don't know exactly what Freddy has planned or, what he's intending to do with this mountain bike. We will use the ropes we had for building the platforms. Myself and Shelia will tie the ropes to ourselves and, all of you will gradually feed the rope to us as we enter the dome. Hopefully, it won't take us long to free Santa but, if it does or, if we get into trouble, I will pull on the rope three times and that will be the signal for help. Has everyone got that?" asked Buddy.

"Yes Buddy," everyone agreed.

"Splendid plan, my old chap." Theodore was being Theodore, of course.

"Just one question, Buddy. Why me?" I asked.

"Because you're the leader of our mission," Buddy answered, making me feel stupid for even asking such a silly question like that.

“Of course, Buddy, no problem. I’ll lead the way,” I said nervously. Buddy and I were now all roped up like horses on a cart. Theodore and the others waited on the platform, all dealing with their own anxieties.

“Good luck!” James shouted at us.

“Thanks!” I yelled back. I knew we were going to need a lot of it. It’s a pity us Irish couldn’t carry a jar of that to use when we need it.

Off we went, like two rock climbers with our ropes. We walked up the toffee steps and crept over the bridge. When we got to the door, the frame was made of metal and there was no door handle. I looked all around for an opening until Buddy came up behind me and just pushed the door forward.

“There you go, Shelia.”

“Thanks Buddy,” I said, once again feeling stupid.

As the door slowly opened, a fog came out, kind of like a witch’s magic potion steaming in a cauldron. We stepped inside the door, which was directly below the bridge. We couldn’t see anything at first, until the fog cleared and there he was. The one man in the world who I had heard about, talked about, imagined but, never believed in. There he was, in human form and my first reaction to seeing this character was nothing. I couldn’t speak. If he was supposed to be a big man with a red suit, white beard and boots, well this wasn’t him. Someone else had Santa and this was a regular old fat guy who had breathing problems.

"Oh, my candy canes, Santa!" Buddy was horrified. "What has Freddy done to you?"

The man slowly lifted his head from the bike he was perched on. "B... B...!" Santa tried to speak.

"It's okay Santa, we are all here and we are going to take you home." Buddy said affectionately

Santa then just spread out on top of the handlebars. It was an awful sight. Freddy had Santa cycling a mountain bike, which looked like it was hooked up to a machine. Santa was weak. He had no suit on but, was wearing a white vest, red shorts and his feet were bare. The dome inside was really hot compared to outside. I thought I was going to pass out. Myself and Buddy stayed strong and helped Santa off the bike, so that he could rest on the floor. We had no water but Mrs Claus had packed a soda bottle inside all of our backpacks so, Buddy gave him a sip. After about ten minutes, Santa started to come around and could see us more clearly.

"Ah! Buddy and Lizzie."

"Actually, Santa, this is Shelia, Lizzie's granddaughter."

"Oh! I'm sorry, Shelia. You are very like your grandmother."

This was it. This was the moment that I was finally going to get answers about why I was here in the North Pole.

"We will have enough time for chatting later. We need to get you out of here," Buddy interrupted. The moment I was waiting for ... gone. Just like that.

"What about the light? I can't leave it here." Santa's voice sounded much better than when we first found him.

"When you feel stronger, we can come back and get it," I said, trying to help.

"Oh, how I wish it was so, little one!"

Who was he calling little? I was almost sixteen and I had led this mission, rather 'finely', as Theodore would say but hey, who was I to start an argument with The Santa Claus?

"Since I have arrived at this mountain, it has been my spirit that's holding it together. Freddy tricked me into thinking I was helping him to melt the mountain but, it wasn't true. Instead, he had managed to create this mountain of ice and a glass dome using the light from my crystal globe. He then forced me to cycle that mountain bike, which he had adapted to take my Christmas spirit. While my spirit was filling the dome, Freddy gradually used it to create this huge ice sculpture. Only now, I'm getting weak. I've been cycling on the bike for more than three days now and, if I release the spirit, it will collapse this whole mountain and we will all be buried under snow. The spirit will be free to wander into many parts of the world, which could have a good or bad effect. I don't want to take that chance." Santa sounded serious.

"Why can't the spirit return to you?" I asked, sounding stupid once again. Why stop then when I was on a roll, right?

"My spirit has not been given to me. It is my belief in Christmas. I don't have doubt or fear. I just believe. Belief alone can do amazing things. With a little food and rest, I'll feel happier and my spirit will shine once more."

Santa was truly someone of importance.

"So, how will we get out of here?" This time I asked a sensible question.

"I must remain here," Santa answered, exhausted.

"Santa, we did not come all this way to leave you here. You are more than just Santa Claus to us elves – you are our father. Christmas is what we do best and, it can never be the same without you," Buddy said sorrowfully.

I'd never seen Buddy like this, he was usually very positive and cheerful. This was a very human side to him. It was like a child helping out his dad. I definitely wasn't expecting any more tears since I had thought James was gone but, I cried like a baby anyway.

"Shelia, why are you crying?" Santa asked.

"Well, it's so sad because, if I couldn't help my father, I would be feeling just like Buddy does now."

"But I haven't finished telling you why I must remain here?"

"Oh! I'm sorry Santa, of course." I felt embarrassed.

"You have an idea?" Buddy asked curiously.

"If I stay here, I can keep an eye on the dome and its spirit levels. You, Shelia and the elves need to get Freddy and bring him to me."

"Ok, Santa but it's going to be tough. That's one grumpy elf," Buddy said to Santa.

"Are the troops here yet?" Santa enquired.

"Yeah, how did you know?" I asked Santa with a suspicious look in my eye.

"They are my personal army. They will follow me and protect me no matter what."

"So why did you ..." I was just about to ask another question and then ...

"Let's go, Shelia. Chit chat later," Buddy cut across me and started to pull on the ropes.

"Ok, I'm coming!" I told Buddy. Then, Santa started to laugh.

We started to make our way back towards the door to the others. The minute James spotted us, he started shouting and cheering.

"Shelia! Buddy! Santa!" When we emerged on our own, Santa-less, his little face dropped.

"Hey, it's okay, James. All is good. Santa is going to be fine. He has decided that he is going to remain inside the dome, to control the spirit levels while we, apparently, have to bring Freddy to him."

"What a splendid idea. We'll go now and get WHO?" Theodore couldn't believe it. "Bring that grumpy old flea to Santa? Excuse my language," Theodore apologised.

"That's what Santa said." Buddy was flabbergasted too.

"So, that could only mean one thing." Theodore held his breath. Then, of course, Ronan couldn't wait to jump in and roll up his sleeves because, he knew what was coming.

"This means war!" Ronan happily declared.

Chapter 13

To Rescue Santa

We started on our long journey back down the stairs. This was my third time. I went first, then Buddy, Theodore, Ronan, Caramel, Sugarsnap, Coco, Pudding, Liam and James. I think we were all a bit anxious about what we were going to see or, who we were going to meet at the bottom. After all, war is not a pretty sight. We gradually descended the stairs, which probably took about thirty minutes. When we got to the bottom, we fell to the ground. Our legs were like jelly.

"How can we win the war with no legs?" Liam asked.

"We use our arms," Pudding replied and they both had a giggle.

"Well, at least someone's having a good time," I remarked.

"It's brilliant, Shelia!" Buddy shouted.

"What is?" I was confused.

"Laughter is brilliant. If we still have our high spirits, we can ..." Buddy said with a sparkle in his eye.

"No ... No ... No ... Not again." I was losing patience.

"Ah come on, Shelia. You know you want to!" Buddy was just taunting me now.

"Ok everyone, this is your leader speaking. Can everyone join hands, close your eyes and be prepared to fly," I said, exhausted.

We all stretched out our little hands, slowly closed our eyes, took a deep breath and before we knew it, we were back on the snowy ground. It was very cold. I'm talking teeth-chattering, body-shivering, nose-sniffling cold. Even though we flew down the mountain to fight a war against Freddy, well the battle had already begun. There were about a hundred elves. All different shapes, colours and sizes. Santa's army had arrived and they were fully loaded. They had candy canes, snowballs, water guns filled with soda, Christmas crackers, sugar bombs and, they even had little machine tanks. This army was fully equipped and not afraid to take down Freddy Freeze. The only problem was, that there was no Freddy to be seen. The elves were fighting a battle with monstrous mountain bikes.

"Sergeant Evergreen, you made it," Buddy called out while the rest of us were still trying to gather our bearings.

"Buddy, old chap. Santa's army, at your service. What's the situation? Have you gained any territory? Where is our target?" The sergeant seemed very cool and organised.

"Allow me!" Theodore spoke up. "At the moment, we have completed the building of a glass dome. Inside, Santa is doing about average but, has managed to keep control of the spirit inside the dome. So far, Santa's orders are as follows:

"Santa will monitor the spirit levels.

"Santa wants Freddy brought to him.

"We, the team on the mission, will help your army to do so.

"We have not gained any territory but, I have made a map of the inside. Santa reckons that this mountain of ice will collapse if we don't tread carefully and, we will all be buried in the snow. Now, Sergeant, it's over to you."

"Affirmative Theodore. There is a place for you, any day, on my squad."

Theodore accepted the compliment with a huge grin on his face.

The sergeant was very army like and very green. He was slightly taller than all the other elves. He was dressed in all-green attire. Even his eyes were green. The sergeant had a strong physique and, unlike the other elves, he wore a green helmet. I could see why he was the leader of Santa's army. He was strong and spoke with authority.

"So, which one of you is in charge of this mission?" the sergeant asked us.

Ronan pushed me forward and I fell flat on my face into the snow, in front of this big elf. If my face wasn't red before, it was now. I was mortified. I jumped to my feet, on my jelly legs, as soon as I could. With a mouthful of snow, I spoke "I am, Sergeant," I was scared.

(I am going to swing for Ronan when I get him home, I thought to myself.)

"Oh, I see. I've never worked with a girl elf in charge but, there is a first time for everything, I suppose. So, what's the mission, eh?" "Shelia is my name," I answered.

"That won't do. I'll call you Captain eh! What's your surname?"

"O'Reilly," I replied.

"Captain O'Reilly it is then. So, what is your mission Captain?" He seemed satisfied with that name.

"To rescue Santa," I slowly answered.

"Well then, it's a good thing you sent for us. I love a good mission and a good battle. The first thing you must do, Captain, is disperse your team. Who is the strongest?"

I looked around at my team with a huge grin on my face. I had forgotten all about getting back at Ronan at home because, now I had him under my command.

"Ronan is the strongest and is not afraid of hard work," I said while staring at Ronan. I bet he wished he had never pushed me now.

"Ok then, Ronan, you will be in the front with myself and Shelia. Grab yourself a water gun from Mighty Munch. He's my right-hand elf.

"Who is next, Captain?" said the sergeant.

Sergeant Evergreen helped me to dispatch my squad. Liam, James and Pudding stayed at the back of the crew. Liam was the lookout while James and Pudding looked after the ammunition of candy-canes, sugar-bombs, snowballs and so on. Caramel, Sugarsnap and Coco were all given candy-canes and toffees to use. The sergeant had his own squad organised and ready. They were all dressed like the Sergeant but, they had normal elf hats on them. Some had beards, some had moustaches, some had long hair and some had short hair but, they were all members of his army. They all knew who was in command.

The sergeant then looked at Theodore,

"We need a plan, Theo. Are you up for the challenge?"

"Sir, yes Sir!" Theodore responded.

"Very good," the sergeant replied and began to give us an update. "Our movements since we arrived are as follows:

"The first thing I saw was the big mountain of ice, sculpted to resemble a mountain bike. We looked all around and noticed the moving pedals. We then, entered the pedals, in two groups of twenty. The other elves remained on the ground to keep a lookout. After we reached the top bar of the bike ..."

"You slipped!" Theodore tried to show off.

"No," said the sergeant who looked confused by Theodore's remark. "We climbed the iron steps leading upwards until we came across a door with a latch. The lock was open so, we pushed the door up and one by one we entered."

"Then, you slipped!" Theodore repeated.

"No," the sergeant replied.

"I'm sorry, Sergeant, continue."

I think, for the first time ever, Theodore felt stupid.

"We didn't get any further. We were only halfway through the door when we heard voices. There was some commotion coming from down on the ground, where the remaining elves stood guard. I couldn't finish exploring, knowing my squad was in trouble so, we returned back down to the ground. Down below, we found five rather large mountain bikes. The bikes were trying to eliminate my troop but, I wasn't having any of it. Since then, it's being us against the bikes. Theodore?"

"Thanks, Sergeant, for the update. It is clear to me that we need to stop the bikes from causing anymore chaos or, it will result in casualties. Did any of you actually see Freddy Freeze?" Theodore asked all the elves.

They all muttered amongst themselves but, none of them had seen Freddy.

"I'm sorry for interrupting but, I can see him and where the bikes have gone," Liam said trembling.

Everyone stopped and looked up. There it was, in all its glory. A robotic type of mountain bike being controlled by none other than Freddy Freeze himself. The contraption was enormous. I thought Freddy was a grumpy elf but, not a cold-hearted one. What was changing him? Freddy was somewhere inside the robot. We couldn't see that far up because, we were only little elves. This thing was the size of my house back in Ireland. The robot was grey and gold in colour. The feet had four small, black tyres on each foot. It looked like a pair of skates. The arms and legs consisted of metal bars and the pedals were the hands. Freddy could easily have scooped us up in them and captured us all. The face of the robot was the saddle turned upwards and it looked like an iron that you would use on clothes. In the chest part of the robot, there was a metal box with a small glass window. It looked as if Freddy was inside there, controlling the robot. Then, we heard his voice. It was no longer just grumpy. It was cold and almost cruel.

"Ah, perfect. Santa's army has arrived. My collection is complete," Freddy announced, like he had some sort of intercom or megaphone. "Listen up, my fellow elves. This is your new commander speaking!"

"Say what? This is outrageous." The sergeant was not pleased about Freddy addressing his squad.

"Put down your weapons and let's have a little chat," said Freddy.

The sergeant didn't like the way Freddy spoke to his troop and he was getting more annoyed.

"Well, look who it is. If it isn't Sergeant Evergreen. The strongest commander in the field. I am very pleased that you have come to visit and I have a proposition for you," said Freddy.

We all started looking around us frantically, not knowing what Freddy was going to say.

"What you see before you is my new factory. It is fully completed with workshops, tools, a top of the range glass dome, Christmas spirit, elves, reindeer and, most importantly, a Santa. And I, Freddy Freeze, would like to invite you and your army to join me here at my new factory.

It just wouldn't be the same without the best fighting squad in the world."

"Well, that's very good of you to say," replied the sergeant.

"Freddy!" Buddy cut in. He could see Freddy was trying to persuade Sergeant Evergreen to join the bad side. "Freddy, it's me, Buddy!" Buddy shouted up to Freddy.

"What? Buddy, aren't you supposed to be busy at work? That dome won't complete itself and I strive for perfection."

"Oh, yes Freddy, the work you set for us has been completed but, there is just one small problem?" said Buddy.

"Alright, whatever it is, make it quick. I'm trying to recruit an army here." Freddy didn't seem to care.

"You see, after we completed the job, we decided to check on Santa." Buddy was now shaking with fear with this enormous robot standing in front of him.

"You did what? How dare you open the dome without my permission? That behaviour will not be tolerated at my factory but, lucky for you, I will give you a second chance. I don't have any other elves and, that is why I'm trying to recruit an army. So, anyway, what's wrong with him? Doesn't like riding a mountain bike, is it?"

"Something like that. He was wondering if he could have a rest and a small chat." Buddy was shaking so much that I thought he was going to faint.

"A small chat, I don't have any time for a chat."

“That’s a bit harsh, don’t you think Freddy?” the sergeant spoke up.

“I don’t see why you care. If your army was so important to him, then why did he pick a bunch of brats, from a country no one has ever heard of, to come rescue him?”

“Hey, that’s rude. You barely know us!” I had to say something because this grumpy elf was getting on my nerves and, if he continued, he was about to get a whole lot of Shelia.

“Well, don’t shoot me. I’m clearly just informing the good sergeant here of the truth. Right, Sergeant?”

“The grump has a point. Why did Santa send for a totally inexperienced troop when he could have had us from the start?” said the sergeant.

All of the elves, who were armed to go into battle, slowly began to drop their weapons. You could hear the soft clatter of candy-canes and water-guns hit the snow. Freddy had worked his cold magic on Sergeant Evergreen and a cold chill ran down my spine. Now we were on our own.

It was like a movie in slow motion. I had to take a deep breath and hope that I wasn’t going to pass out. I gazed around at the scene in front of me. I wasn’t dreaming anymore. Everything was real. I was in the North Pole, chosen to save Santa. Everything that I witnessed tonight was rushing through my head. Then, a feeling came over me. A feeling of belief that I never thought existed came up through me, like a volcano. If I was a fiery volcano, well, then let the lava flow and melt this ice cream cone.

"Now, just hold on there one minute, Freddy. Santa loves everyone and treats us all equally. He did not leave his army behind and chose a bunch of nobodies to rescue him. No, sergeant, he didn't. This mission began for reasons close to Santa's heart. Number one was you, Freddy. Santa came here to make amends, if you had just let him speak. Number two was me, Shelia O'Reilly: I never believed in Santa Claus."

I told them all with such a sorrowful feeling. The elf army gasped. I even think Freddy was shocked.

"Yeah, I know. It's shocking but true. Santa brought me here to teach me the true meaning of Christmas. Ronan, Liam and James, I'm sorry for everything I've ever said or done that wasn't nice. If you can forgive me, I will try my hardest to be less bossy."

"Shelia, you're our only sister. We love you even when you're bossy" Ronan answered back.

"Especially when you're bossy," Liam joined in and James gave me a huge hug.

My eyes started to well up with tears but, I had to stop them because my volcanic eruption was not over. When I turned back, all of the elves were staring at us with admiration.

"Where was I? Eh, number three, Santa wants to get Christmas back on track. Freddy, the world will not be the same with all of this wickedness. So what? You are a little on the grumpy side but yet, look around: your fellow elves, your family is here. I mean Buddy, Caramel, Coco, Sugarsnap, Theodore and Pudding. You should see the amazing work they have done on the glass dome and never once did they complain. They did it because you, their brother, asked them to. If you could find it in your heart to just come out of your robot, which by the way, is super cool, we can put everything right."

Ok, now that I had finished my ramble, I could breathe and hope he did the right thing.

"But, but, what if I don't want to come out? I have everything I need so, why doesn't everyone come to the cold side? You can be my ... my Snow Patrol. Your first command will be to help me build snow mobiles. Each member of the Snow Patrol will have a snow mobile for transport and, they will have the best weapons ever," said Freddy trying his best to convince them to join his side.

The elves' faces lit up. Who would blame them? It was like a child at Christmas getting a toy bike to play with, while his friend got the real thing. It was jealousy at full force and Freddy was riding the bike higher and higher up the mountainside. The elves started whispering amongst themselves. They were actually considering Freddy's offer. Then, the volcano began to erupt again.

"Now, that's not fair Freddy! Can't you at least please come down?" I was getting impatient.

"I've thought about it and, no. So, what are you going to do about it?" Freddy started to sound wicked again. I knew this couldn't be good.

"Psst! Sheila, over here!" I heard my name being called from behind me. I looked back and Buddy, Ronan and Theodore were in deep conversation.

"Listen Shelia, I hope that I'm wrong but, I don't think Freddy is open to negotiation. Do you remember Santa saying that Christmas spirit can be bad or good?"

"Yeah!" I replied slowly.

"Well, I think Freddy has used the spirit to do bad and, it is now affecting his soul. He is becoming mean and wicked and, I think it's only Santa who can save him now," said Buddy.

"Alright, so, what can we do?" I asked. I was exhausted from all the heartfelt speeches.

"There's nothing you can do for now but, I need to speak to Sergeant Evergreen," Buddy gulped.

"Hey, Sergeant Evergreen. Sir, do you mind if I have a word with you?" Sergeant Evergreen nodded.

"I know you may feel like Santa has betrayed you and that joining Freddy in his quest to be the Ice King, or whatever, may seem exciting but, Santa didn't betray you. Santa was only trying to bring Christmas cheer to everyone and right now, he's not looking too good. Santa has been forced to stay in a glass dome in extreme heat and he is losing his spiritual power. He needs all our help because, that's what we do – we help those in need. Now, you and Shelia have a chance to rescue Santa and spread Christmas cheer all over the world again. Santa can help Freddy and, you never know, he might return home with us and still make those snow mobiles that you like. What do you say?"

Buddy was wearing his heart on his sleeve and was hoping to gain Sergeant Evergreens support.

"Do you know what, Buddy? You're right! I'm sorry for nearly abandoning you and our mission. And I'm very sorry, Captain O'Reilly. Please forgive my troop and myself for such idiotic thinking. We got distracted with material things. There is only one man we take orders from and that's Santa."

"You are forgiven and now it's time for action. Theodore, what's the plan?" I said, all ready for action.

Freddy stayed inside his robot while all of the battle discussions were going on down below. The troop picked their weapons up and began to regroup. Myself, Ronan, Buddy, Theodore, Sergeant Evergreen and Mighty Munch put our heads together.

"What's the plan, Theo?" the sergeant asked.

"Our main aim, at this point in time, is Freddy. We need to bring down that robot so that Freddy will feel defenceless."

"No problem, Theo. What's our strategy?" Sergeant Evergreen was a true military leader. I felt so embarrassed standing next to him.

"There is one strategy but, I do not wish to say," said Theodore. Ronan then decided to say it for him. (Please don't let him say something stupid, please! I was cringing at the thought of Ronan's contribution.)

"I'll say it. Let's go and kick some robotic circuits."

"Why, thank you, kind fellow. That's exactly how I would put it."

"Listen up, everybody!" Theodore continued to explain his plan.

"Freddy's robot has tyres. So, I say let's launch everything we've got at the wheels. Candy-canes, sugar-bombs, snowballs, you name it. Throw the bells at the end of your boots if you have to. Once the robot loses its grip, it should come crashing down. Liam will be our lookout. If there is any sign of the robot tilting, you must shout 'stop' at the top of your voice. Are you okay with that order?"

"Yes, sir," Liam replied and saluted like he was a real soldier.

Next, Pudding and James were put in charge of ammunition.

"If you're running low, let Mighty Munch know."

"Shelia, Buddy, Ronan, Sergeant Evergreen and I, will need full water-guns. The only thing Freddy's afraid of is getting wet. When we bring him down, I'm hoping we could use it to make him surrender. Now this is the only strategy I have so, it better work."

"Good plan, Theo, good plan," the sergeant remarked. "Now, my troop, grab everything you can get a hold of and take your positions."

Buddy looked at me and whispered, "Are you ready?"

"I'm fully loaded and ready to roll."

"On my count everyone. One, two, three ... charge," instructed Sergeant Evergreen. The battle began.

We all ran as fast as we could in the snow. There was screaming and shouting that sounded just like ninjas. I have to admit, it was a little exciting. All of the weaponry, including candy canes and toffees, were thrown at the robot. Freddy tried his best to control the robot but, it wasn't working. The wheels were rolling back and forth continuously. Whenever he managed to get a grip, another candy cane would get stuck under the wheel. We could hear a lot of grumpy muttering going on up above.

"Leave me alone. Get out of my home," Freddy shouted at us.

It didn't look like Freddy had tested his own device. He was shifting gears and pressing buttons frantically. The arms and legs were moving all over the place until ... 'STOP'. We heard the warning call and we ran like our lives depended on it. We were scared because, we didn't know if the robot would land on top of us and crush us.

"Run! Run!" I could hear Liam, James and Pudding shouting.

Then, there was a huge bang. The force of the robot falling down made it feel like there was an earthquake. The loose ice came at us like dust. It felt like frost had stuck to us. Everything stood still and it was quiet. Then, I could hear a creak coming from the robot. I looked up and, there he stood. This little grumpy figure. He lost his hat and you could see his wispy grey hair. He was dizzy and stumbled out of the door at the back of the robot. Freddy looked around him, confused.

"Is there anybody out there?" he called.

With the force of the robot coming down, we were all covered in ice. Freddy couldn't see any of us from where he was standing because, well, let's face it, this thing was huge, even lying face down.

"I've done it. I have committed an awful act. I have killed all of my fellow elves and I don't know why. I'm a terrible elf."

Then, I could hear it. A little whimper. I rose to my feet and swept away the ice. I could see Freddy, standing on the edge. He was crying. We did it. We had stopped Freddy. I could feel a relief in my heart and my lava was starting to cool down. All the other elves began to emerge from the snow. Freddy remained where he was, weeping. We all looked at each other, relieved. We were all okay but, we couldn't help but feel bad for Freddy. How could this very talented elf have let his life go down this road?

Freddy didn't notice any of us surrounding him as he held his face in his hands. Then, Buddy climbed up the robot to Freddy.

"Freddy! Freddy! It's me, Buddy!"

"Wait a minute. Who said that?" Freddy sniffled.

He turned around and, lo and behold, Buddy stood there. Freddy slowly rose to his feet and took one glance at Buddy. He ran towards him and gave him a big hug.

"Welcome back, Freddy!" Buddy said to him.

"But, I thought you were all ..." Freddy was trembling.

"Now, now. None of that talk anymore. Freddy, you are alive. We all are."

"It's a Christmas miracle!" Freddy announced.

"No Freddy, it's Christmas spirit," Buddy replied.

"Oh no! Santa!" Freddy exclaimed.

"He's all alone in that glass dome, probably ..."

"No, we've seen that he is okay. A little dehydrated and weak but, otherwise cheerful."

"Thank you, Buddy. Thank you, Sergeant. Thank you, Shelia and thank you, everyone. I gave up my spirit to go on a journey of madness but, you all saved me. I will never forget it."

"You know what this means?" shouted Pudding.

Then, they all broke out in song.

"Ding! Dong! Christmas is here, so let's all cheer, Christmas is here. Ding! Dong! Christmas cheer is here."

Ok, I know we shouldn't have because, technically, we weren't elves but, myself, Ronan, Liam and James joined in. Buddy caught my eye and saluted me. I saluted back.

With our mini celebration complete, we all gathered together and went to rescue Santa. Back up the stairs we went for the last time. I didn't ever want to see those stairs again. Sergeant Evergreen and his troop remained down below on patrol. Buddy, Ronan, Liam, James, Theodore, Caramel, Coco, Sugarsnap, Pudding and myself all made the dreaded journey again but, this time Freddy joined us.

Chapter 14

A Favour to Ask

Our spirits were all high and now, we were continuing on with our mission. We reached the top of the stairs and we rushed to see Santa but, there was a problem. The toffee had melted and the iron grates had become loose.

"How can we get Santa out?" Buddy asked Freddy, rather worried.

"I don't know; I thought you fixed it," Freddy replied.

"But you built the glass dome, right? So, how did you get Santa in there?" Buddy asked Freddy, hoping there was a logical explanation.

"Well, you see, I kind of used all of the power I had on building the mountain and the glass dome. When Santa arrived looking for me, I was in the middle of creating the glass dome and he tried to stop me. Santa leaped forward from the stairway and landed right inside the dome. There was no way out for him but, I flew out. I came out and continued on to create the mountain bike and a bridge for an entrance. I knew the only way that I could succeed with my own factory was to have more power. I know I shouldn't have but, I made Santa cycle the bike as to drain every last drop of his spirit. I know

now that it was wrong of me but, the idea of having all the power makes you do crazy things."

"Well, that has to be the answer. We could fly in," Buddy said.

"But how will we come back out?" Theodore was asking a sensible question.

"I don't know but, maybe Santa will. So, what do you say, Shelia?" Buddy asked me.

Everyone now looked at me because, it wasn't a big secret that I didn't like flying. "Ok Buddy, we'll fly!" I replied.

Myself, Buddy and Freddy went to check on Santa, while the others remained behind.

"How about we try to finish the job perfectly this time," Theodore announced to everyone.

They all agreed. So off myself, Buddy and Freddy flew. We went inside the mystical door again and saw Santa. He was standing up, looking at the spirit levels and sipping on some hot chocolate that we had left him. When he heard us come in, he turned his head to see who it was.

"Shelia! Buddy! And Freddy! I'm so glad to see you."

"Santa!" Buddy cheered and ran to give him a big hug.

"Oh! Is everyone else too big to give me a hug?" Santa looked at me and Freddy.

I went over slowly, step by step, and Santa gave me a big squeeze. It was warm and magical. Freddy stood there, looking at the ground, shuffling his feet.

"Freddy, come over and talk to me," Santa said to Freddy with such a gentle voice.

Santa scooped Freddy up in his arms and gazed at him lovingly. Freddy looked into Santa's eyes.

"I'm sorry. I should never have left my home and stolen from you. I guess, I got the idea in my head that you didn't want me so, you were sending me away to the cold mountains."

"Ho! Ho! Ho! Freddy, I love all my elves equally, even if they seem a bit grumpy. That shows you have character and without you, the toy factory would not be the same. I'm sorry, Freddy, for ever letting you think that I didn't want you. I was only sending you off to test the mountain bikes and instead, you managed to accomplish this sculpture."

"Eh, guilty again, Santa," Freddy admitted. "I used all of the spirit that I stole to make the mountain bike and the glass dome."

"I know about the stolen spirit but, surely you sculpted them with your heart."

"Well, actually I did. I just wanted a perfect home and factory for myself. Does that seem selfish?"

"No, Freddy. You love your work and everyone needs a home but tonight, you are coming back to your real home, with your real family."

"But, if you leave the mountain, everything will collapse and I can't bear that," Freddy sounded sad.

"No, Freddy, it won't. Not once you have used some of your own spirit to make it."

"But we did!"

We could now hear shouting and cheering coming from the door. It was Theodore, Ronan, Caramel, Coco, Sugarsnap, Pudding, Liam and James.

"We completed the dome entrance and it looks rather jolly good," Theodore said, happily.

Then, all the elves ran and smothered Santa with hugs.

"You see, Freddy, everything has worked out the way you planned it."

"Not really, Santa, I must confess. I tried not only to steal your spirit but, your elves and army too!"

"And have you learned anything from your mistakes?" Santa asked Freddy.

"Not to mess with Sergeant Evergreen's army because, they will take you down," replied Freddy with a sense of humour.

"Freddy?" Santa repeated.

"Ok, ok. Don't use Christmas spirit badly because others can get hurt and bad Christmas cheer can affect the whole world."

"Exactly!" replied Santa.

"But Santa, if you can forgive me, I would like to ask you for a favour."

"Sure, anything, Freddy."

"Can you stop me from feeling so grumpy and angry? I don't want to be as wicked as I have been until now."

"That's a strange request but consider it done. Come here to me. Give me your hands, close your eyes and breathe in and out slowly."

Then, there it was – a Christmas miracle.

Santa was going to turn Freddy Freeze into Freddy Defrost. Santa held on to Freddy's hands and he lit up like fairy lights on a Christmas tree. Freddy then opened his eyes and looked around.

"How will I know if it worked?" he asked Santa.

"Well, I'm not sure. Do you feel anyway less wicked?" asked Santa.

"No!" Freddy replied.

"I know," Theodore cut in.

"Why don't you go out of the dome and check on the entrance we finished?"

"Ok, I don't see how this will test how my wicked feelings are now." Freddy was unsure of Theodore's idea.

"Just trust me, Freddy, I know everything and everyone," said Theodore.

Freddy slowly walked up to the entrance and all of a sudden, we could hear him.

"That just won't do! The bridge isn't in line with the iron grates, there is sugar stuck everywhere and, what do you call that over there? That's not a platform but a death trap." Freddy rambled on.

"And there you have it, a perfectly grumpy Freddy. Am I a genius or what?" Theodore said smugly.

"What," answered Pudding.

Everyone began to laugh. Theodore just gave him the you're-the-annoying-little-brother look.

"So, what do you say to getting home and starting some celebrations?" Buddy asked everyone.

"That sounds good," Santa replied, "but, just one more thing before we leave – you don't suppose anyone has a spare jacket and trousers?"

"I will go and ask Freddy," Buddy said and off he went.

"Eh Santa?"

"Yes Ronan!"

"What will you do with the mountain?" Ronan asked.

"I have decided to leave it here as a new project for Freddy. It would be such a shame to melt it."

"Freddy! Freddy! Could you come in here for a moment?" Santa called Freddy to ask him about his idea.

"Yes, Santa, you called!" Freddy came back inside the dome.

"Before we leave, Freddy, I wanted to ask you, what do you plan on doing with your new project?"

"Eh ... my new project," Freddy was confused. "What new project?"

"This magnificent mountain bike sculpture."

"But I thought you would want to melt it."

Freddy was surprised that Santa wanted to keep the mountain bike.

"Well, apart from creating my own North Pole and factory, I had wanted to specialise in suitable snow toys and machines. The first thing on my list was snow mobiles for your army," said Freddy.

"Well, that sounds like a lot of work."

Freddy hung his head, thinking Santa didn't have any confidence in his ideas.

"But, I'm sure Sergeant Evergreen and his troop will be more than happy to help you." Santa smiled at Freddy.

"Do you think?" Freddy asked excitedly now.

"Why don't you ask them?"

And Freddy was gone like a shot. Buddy just so happened to be coming back at the same time and Freddy nearly knocked him over.

"I'm back, Santa and here's your suit, as you requested. Where is Freddy going?" Buddy asked when his eyes stopped rolling in his head.

"Freddy is going to start a factory for making toys that are suitable for snow and, he has gone to ask the elf army if they would like to help."

"Toys that are durable in snow. That sounds pretty co...ool!" Buddy replied, pretending to shiver. Everyone began to laugh and for some reason, it didn't feel as cold anymore.

"How are we going to get back home in time for Christmas?" Buddy asked.

"Well, Rudolph and Prancer of course," Theodore answered.

"Well, I don't suppose you know where they are, Theodore the genius?" said Buddy.

"Down the stairs, third room on the left," replied Theodore sharply.

"How do you know that?" Buddy asked.

I saw a door marked 'Reindeer Shelter' when we came in.

"Oh!" said Buddy. "Well done you for noticing."

"Thank you, Buddy," Theodore answered back.

"So, what do you say we get this show on the snow?" I said without thinking how lame it sounded.

"Seriously, Shelia!" remarked Ronan.

"Let's go! Let's go! Let's go!" James started getting excited.

"Hey, calm down, there firecracker. We don't want you falling again," I grabbed James to stop him from running on ahead of us.

"But we're going to meet Santa's reindeer."

"I know but, we're in no hurry. Take your time."

"You just don't want to fly again," Liam cut in.

"Ok, you got me, guilty as charged. Lock me up and throw away the key."

James and Liam just gave me a long look, not knowing what I was talking about.

"There is nothing more for you to worry about, Shelia. Christmas spirit has filled you up and there is nothing that you don't believe in," said Buddy.

Chapter 15

Goodbyes

We all headed off to find Rudolph and Prancer. The elves were singing Christmas songs and everyone was in high spirits. Theodore, of course, was correct. Third room on the left was where we found the reindeer, who seemed to be in perfect health. Freddy had given them plenty of food and drink, had cotton capes draped over them, had fairy lights hung all over the room and had spread out straw for their beds. Santa and the elves were pleased to see them.

“Shelia, Ronan, Liam and James, I would like you to meet my very trustee reindeer,” Santa Introduced us, “Rudolph and Prancer.”

“Wow, they’re beautiful creatures. I would love to have reindeer back on the farm,” Ronan said, loving every moment of this. Cows, goats, sheep, pigs, horses, chickens: that’s his world.

“They are very beautiful, Ronan, but don’t let them fool you. They can throw their antlers about like any child having a tantrum,” Santa told Ronan.

“Oh, I know that only too well!” Sugarsnap exclaimed. “One time, I decided to borrow some of Rudolph’s apples to make some candy apples. Big mistake! Let's just say, I couldn't sit down for a week."

All the elves began to giggle.

"It wasn't funny!" Sugarsnap snapped. I even think Rudolph was sniggering at her.

"Can I pet him?" James asked like any child at a pet shop.

"Of course," replied Santa. "Just be careful of the antlers."

Everyone glanced at Sugarsnap again.

"Ok, laugh it up but next time I make candy apples, I'm not sharing," Sugarsnap scoffed and folded her arms.

"It's okay Sugarsnap, I'm sure they will be the best candy apples in the world." She gave Santa a little wink of her eye and whispered, "You and Mrs Claus can have one."

"So, Theodore, is the sleigh in one of the other rooms?" Santa asked.

"Yes, Santa, it is in the room next door marked, 'modes of transportation'."

"Very good," Santa praised him. "I don't think this mission would have been complete without your cleverness."

Theodore stood up with his head held high. Santa and the elves, with Ronan and myself, pushed the sleigh out of the room, while Liam and James stayed, admiring the famous reindeer.

“I don’t suppose you know the way out?” Buddy looked at Theodore while we were all panting and pushing. This thing must have weighed a tonne.

“There’s a trapdoor at the side of the reindeer’s shelter. All we have to do is saddle up the reindeer and away we go,” Theodore was panting as he replied.

Seriously, it was like pushing a really stubborn elephant.

We got the sleigh back to the reindeer’s shelter and the elves did their magic. They had Rudolph and Prancer saddled up in no time. Santa decided he wanted to head down to the ground and check on Freddy and his army. Myself, Ronan, Buddy and Theodore went with him. The other elves remained behind with Liam and James. You couldn’t pry them away from the animals, even for a minute. When Santa’s army caught a glimpse of Santa, they began to cheer. I think even Sergeant Evergreen had a tear in his eye. The troops crawled all over Santa like ants.

“Commander, you have been rescued and you will now return home to complete Christmas.”

“Yes, I have, Sergeant, thanks to you, your troops and my elite team.”

“He’s talking about us,” Theodore whispered.

“I believe Freddy here has a very exciting project for you all,” Santa announced.

“Yes, Commander, he has explained and we have agreed. I think this could be a very successful operation, once it is up and running,” the sergeant replied.

"I don't doubt it. I think Freddy here has shown us his worth. So, what do you all say to returning back home and getting the party started?" Santa asked excitedly.

The sergeant didn't reply and Freddy held his head down. The troops were still behaving like ants.

"Santa, as much as I appreciate your forgiveness and my second chance so much ..." Freddy said, looking at his feet again. "But, if you don't mind, I would like to remain behind and fix the mess I created."

Freddy pointed to the broken robot. "I will also be able to get a start on the new factory."

Santa looked at the robot and was surprised.

"Wow, would you look at that?" said Santa when he saw the huge robot lying motionless on the ice.

"If you are dedicated to the project, then who am I to stop your enthusiasm? But you don't have any survival supplies."

"We have!" replied the sergeant. "We would be more than happy to stay with Freddy and begin our new project."

"But what about our celebrations?" Buddy said sorrowfully.

"We need our whole family to have a party."

"Buddy, you have such a good heart but, you are forgetting one thing. Freddy and Santa's army will always be members of our family and, when they complete their work, we will welcome them home and it will be another reason for a party. But, right now, we have new members of our extended family.

What Shelia and her brothers have done for us is definitely worth celebrating, don't you think?"

Buddy wiped away the tears from his eyes and leaped into the air. "You're right, Santa, off we go!"

"Santa? I will always remember what you did for me and I can assure you, I will make you proud," Freddy looked up at Santa now with confidence.

"I know you will," replied Santa in his caring fatherly voice. Santa then gave Freddy and the ants a big hug.

"Don't worry, Commander, I'll keep an eye on Freddy!" Sergeant Evergreen said with authority.

"Thank you, Sergeant. I have great belief in you all but for now, I must bid you all farewell."

"And I will come with more supplies for you tomorrow," Buddy added.

"Goodbye, little ones!" Santa boomed out over the troops with his big Santa Claus voice.

"Goodbye, dear Santa!" they all cheered back.

It was all very emotional. We all climbed back up the dreaded mountain again, to get the reindeer and to find the others. Between Sugarsnap, Coco, Caramel, Pudding, Liam and James, they had done a pretty good job.

"Everyone climb on board," Santa called out.

We all scrambled to get the best spot. If anything, I only wanted a corner to curl up in and sleep. Buddy let down the trapdoor and came back to the sleigh.

"Is everybody ready?" Santa called out.

"Yeah!" we all called back to Santa.

"On Rudolph, on Prancer, on up we go!" Santa called out. "Ho! Ho! Ho! Merry Christmas."

And then there was a strange magical sound, like jingle bells ringing in the air. We all waved goodbye to Freddy, Sergeant Evergreen and the troops. They waved back. The jingle bell sounds rang out all the way back to the toy factory. I was never going to get any sleep.

Chapter 16

Sweets and Strawberries

We flew through the air for twenty minutes or so and then, we could see the toy factory again. I saw the sugar heaven palace but, I didn't mind this time. I was really hungry now. We didn't need to ring any doorbell or knock on the door. It was almost as if Santa's jingle bell sounds automatically opened it and, we flew through and landed in the middle of the corridor. Then, the reaction of the elves was like a musical. Every elf in the factory came running to see Santa and they were all as high as kites with happiness.

"Greetings, my treasures, slow down, don't knock me down," Santa said playfully.

The elves came and surrounded us all, shaking hands, giving us hugs, patting us on the back and telling us, "well done" and "thank you".

"Hey everyone! Let's get inside and celebrate!" Buddy shouted.

"And eat," Ronan muttered under his breath.

Typical, you can't bring him anywhere without him complaining of hunger but hey, I love my sleep and food too so, I suppose we are one as bad as the other.

We entered a different room than the last time we were here, being guided by the elves. It was the best party ever! There were red and gold streamers hung all over the room. There were balloons of every colour. There was a chocolate fountain with marshmallows, stacks of toffees, fudges, bon bons (my favourite), jelly babies and white chocolate buttons (James's favourite). There was an endless amount of biscuits to cookies, custard creams, jammy dodgers and chocolate digestives (Liam's favourite). Then, there was a soda fountain. Every two minutes, the flavour changed. You had cola, orange, lemonade and fizzy apple. I can't believe I'm going to say this but, "yummy".

When you passed all the luxurious treats on tables, you then got to the end where the most important treat of any party was laid. It was the CAKE! I had to stop my eyes from popping out of my head and wipe the drool from my mouth. It was humongous. There were at least (AT LEAST!) twelve tiers, starting from the biggest at the bottom to the smallest at the top. It was covered in white buttercream and decorated with strawberries and, wait a minute ... strawberries and not sweets. That's a surprise. Mrs Claus stood beside the cake. Her smile was beaming from ear to ear when she caught a glimpse of Santa. He too smiled back and they shared a big hug.

"Welcome home," Mrs Claus whispered to him.

"It's good to be home," he whispered. "So, what are we waiting for? Where's the entertainment?" Santa enquired.

"Right here, Santa!" A group of elves ran over to an empty table and they all had little toy instruments. They played away until their hearts were content and we got a free Christmas concert.

As everyone was munching away and listening to the little elf band, I noticed Santa slipping away from the party. I knew my brothers were too busy having fun to notice if I was gone. Santa was so fast, I was out of breath trying to catch up with him. He went out the front door and I went in pursuit. I nearly got caught in the door but, I managed to squeeze through just in time before it closed. Santa walked across the snow in the direction of his house.

(Oh no, how am I supposed to get across the snow? I can't go back inside either, now that the door is closed. Think, Shelia, think. I only know one way but, I don't like it. I'll have to fly!)

I closed my eyes and off I flew.

CHAPTER 17

The Missing List

Santa went into his house and closed the door and then, what did Shelia do? I opened my eyes and bang! Right into the front door. Please say he didn't hear me.

"Hello? Who's there?" Santa called out.

(Good one, Shelia, I thought to myself. I'd never make it as a spy.)

"It's only me, Santa! It's Shelia."

"Shelia! What brings you here?" Santa replied curiously.

He knew exactly why I was there. He just wanted me to admit I was nosey. Santa opened the door and I walked in hanging my head.

"So, what's bugging you, little one?"

It was as if he knew exactly what I was thinking.

"Well, you see, I was kind of wondering if you have the time since you are so busy..." Santa started laughing with a glint in his eyes.

"Could you tell me how you know my grandmother?" He started to laugh even louder and, believe it or not, his belly shook like a bowl of jelly.

"Ho! Ho! Ho! Is that the only question you have?" he asked.

"Well there are a few more."

"Well, ask away." Santa kicked off his boots, lay back in his chair and sat me on his knee.

"Did my grandmother help you? What was she like? Do you know my mother? Did she help you? Why don't we ever get to see you? Why do all your elves have funny names? Why do they eat a lot of sugar? Why did you choose me and my brothers to help you? Was this like a test or, am I dreaming? When will I wake up and when will I be going home?" I asked my questions really fast, until I was out of breath. Santa just smiled and began to tell me the answers.

"Yes, Shelia, I did know your grandmother. She was just like you. When she was a little girl, she gave up on Christmas. Her spirit was broken so, I decided that she should come and help me."

"So, it was like a test," I interrupted.

Santa looked down at me and smiled.

"I'm sorry, do continue," I said, slightly embarrassed.

"It was the Christmas of 1929 and I had lost my Christmas 'naughty and nice' list. The elves and I searched everywhere. We must have turned the toy factory and this house upside down looking for it. So, I decided we needed help from the outside. The elves and I had been working so hard getting all the toys ready that, we forgot which names went on which present. When I went to check the office where I keep my list, I discovered it was gone. The place turned from calm into chaos. Every elf was tearing through the whole office and factory but, no joy.

"Then, I sent for your grandmother, Lizzy. When we met first, she was a bit like ... well, Freddy. Grumpy and didn't want to speak with anyone. One year, she was on the naughty list and didn't receive a present from me. From that day forward, she became more grumpy and angry. She didn't make friends easily. Enter Buddy. Buddy flew her here to the North Pole and she had a ball and made not one, not two but more than five hundred friends. It turned out that messy fingers Pudding had accidently wiped his hands with the list and had put it in the bin. Lizzy questioned all the elves like a real detective and retraced all their steps. After about eight hours, we located the paper, cleaned it off and did the best we could to make out the names.

"From her adventure, your grandmother regained her Christmas spirit and vowed to teach her own children all about Christmas."

"So, that would explain why my mother is always is in high spirits."

"Precisely and now, she's passing it on to you and your brothers."

"Wow, I was not expecting that," I said to Santa.

"It is true and now, I have brought you here to do the same. I wanted you to experience your Christmas spirit once again. Let me ask you, why did you stop believing?"

"Probably because I overheard a group of girls at school saying that Santa wasn't real and, well, it broke my heart. I always enjoyed Christmas until, they ruined it for me."

"Your spirit is within you and no one else. You just needed to ignite it again, that's all."

"And what about my brothers?" I asked.

"I wanted you to understand the closeness of families. Liam and James are high in Christmas spirit but Ronan ... he's afraid."

Santa surprised me with that.

"Oh no, that's not Ronan. He's afraid of nothing but the cold," I said proudly. (Yes, I was actually proud of Ronan.)

"He's afraid of disappointment. He keeps his guard up, like an Alsatian, so as to avoid getting hurt. If he keeps his guard up, how can he love, hope, wish or even believe?"

It was all starting to make sense.

"When you return home, maybe you could find a way to put him on the right path," Santa suggested to me.

Then, thinking about how I was going to explain this adventure when I got home, never mind trying to help Ronan, I asked, "Won't he just remember today? Will that not help him?"

"I'm sorry but, this adventure was for you and we managed to help Freddy too so, that was a bonus," Santa replied.

"So, my brothers won't remember anything at all?" I felt kind of sad.

"No, they will have some memory of it but, they will think it was a dream – all part of a story that you told them."

"Ah! Clever," I gave Santa a nod.

Then it hit me. "I've just thought of a plan for Ronan," I said to Santa.

"That's the spirit! Theodore must have had an effect on you," Santa exclaimed.

"He did, in a strange way. He kind of reminds me of my Aunt Helen only, he's more intelligent. Don't tell him I said that."

Santa laughed.

"So, just how was it that you named all your elves?" I was starting to feel really comfortable with Santa now.

"Oh, that was down to the parents. They let their Christmas spirit guide them I suppose," replied Santa.

"Well, I know Pudding likes to make and eat pudding, Sugarsnap loves sugar and candies, Caramel Coffee loves the combination of caramel and coffee, Coco loves chocolate. What about Buddy and Theodore?" I asked.

"Theodore Truffle loves truffles. He's the one with expensive tastes and Buddy – I thought you would have worked that one out by now," Santa gave me a look that said, "Think about it."

So, I thought about it. "Buddy, Buddy, I've got it, its friendship," I shouted out.

Santa laughed at me, "Well done."

"There are even twin elves called turtle and dove. Their mother explained to me that one walks slowly like a turtle and the other is quiet and peaceful, like a dove."

"Wow!" was all I could say.

"What will happen when we return home?" I continued with my never-ending questions.

"You may all feel tired for a little while but, nothing a good meal and a night's sleep won't fix," Santa replied.

"Right now, that sounds like Heaven," I said.

"So, what's with all the sugar?"

"The elves love it but, I'm a strawberry person myself."

Well, that explains the cake.

"Will I ever be able to return and visit the North Pole?" I asked cheekily, knowing well what the answer was going to be.

"Do you like to fly?" Santa asked me, knowing what the answer would be.

"No!" I answered, "but, I would like to see you and the elves again."

"That won't be possible. If the truth be told, if I remain a mystery to the world, then people will continue to hope, wish and believe. On the other hand, if I reveal myself to the world, people's demands and expectations will be too much and I will become a joke. I will be just another marketing idea. The spirit I have seen being spread all over the world will be gone in the blink of an eye. Parents will be put under great pressure to keep their children happy but, I tell you now, it will not work. It will create a wicked world of greed. That's the purpose of keeping our good spirit alive."

Well, I was speechless.

The story Theodore had told us earlier made sense.

"I have something for you, Shelia. Call it a little thank you from us all here in the North Pole." Santa gave me a tiny red box.

"Go ahead and have a look," he said.

Inside, there was a silver necklace. It had a little crystal ball on the end. It was a replica of Santa's crystal ball with the globe of the world inside. I put it on immediately.

"Every time you need a little guidance, hold on to the crystal, close your eyes and take a deep breath. Anything troubling you will become a lot easier."

This was not a 'thank you' gift. It was a special, one-of-a-kind gift and Santa had given it to me.

"I am honoured to receive such a gift. Thank you, Santa."

"So, what do you say to getting back to the party or, do you have any more questions?"

"I've got no more questions, Santa. I have everything I need in here." I held on to my necklace, closed my eyes, took a deep breath and I was ready.

Santa and I returned to the celebrations. The party was in full swing and no one had even noticed we were gone. Liam and James were dancing a jive (Yes, a jive!) with girl elves. Ronan was showing off to the others by telling how he took Freddy down all by himself. Oh, boys, they'll never grow up. Always want to impress. Mrs Claus then noticed us and came over.

"Where did you two get to then?" she asked.

"We just had a little business to take care of but, it's sorted now," Santa winked at me.

"Why don't you go and enjoy yourself before you go home."

"Yes, please. I've had my eyes on that cake since we got back."

I ran over as fast as my legs could carry me. I took a plate and spoon. I scooped out a big piece, just for myself. I wolfed it down. I had frosting on my nose and the strawberries were so juicy that the juice ran down my chin. This was the best cake I ever had. I wondered if Mrs Claus would give me the recipe. As I was busy with my head in the cake, I heard the music stopping and Santa's voice.

"Can I have everyone's attention please? I would just like to say a big thanks to all my treasures who helped get Christmas back on track. Every year, you all give me one hundred and ten per cent and never let me down. I thought that you should all know that Freddy did something that wasn't very wise of him but, he has since changed for the better. Freddy and Sergeant Evergreen have decided to stay behind and finish a new project. So, we shall be in the business of making durable snow toys."

"Wow, that's great!" all the elves cheered and applauded.

"I also have a very special thank you I would like to extend to a special family: Shelia, Ronan, Liam and James, your bravery and determination has shown us your worth. You really and truly are a special family. I hope you will always keep your faith in Christmas and in each other."

Then, all the elves applauded for us. I could feel my face going red with embarrassment. Ronan, of course, stood there like a prize stallion with his head in the air and Liam and James were ... they were fast asleep. Snoring their little heads off. They didn't hear a word Santa had said. Everyone started giggling when they saw the pair of them sucking their thumbs.

"It looks like those two have had enough excitement for one night," I said to Santa. "I think it's time for home."

"Awe!" None of the elves wanted us to leave.

"Now there, my little treasures, we ourselves have a lot of work ahead of us tomorrow," Santa reminded them.

"And I have to check in on Freddy and the troops," Buddy added.

"Shelia, you have completed your mission and for that, we thank you and relieve you of your service. It is time to send you all home."

"Thank you for having us," I replied.

"Buddy you will see them home safely?" Santa asked.

"Yes Santa!" Buddy replied without any signs of exhaustion, which is more than could be said for me.

Santa gathered us together. All of the elves waved goodbye and wished us good luck. We held hands, closed our eyes and, off we flew. This time with more exciting memories than ever before.

Chapter 18

The Following Morning

We landed back in our little home in Mayo. The room was exactly as we had left it. There were sheets thrown all over the place. It still had a hint of magic about it. Ronan, Liam and James lay back in their beds. Buddy held up his little hands and, it was like a warm summer breeze had spread through the house. The once magical scene was now back to a normal bedroom. I looked up at the clock and it was 7am. The harsh winter cold that we had been experiencing for the last couple of days was beginning to thaw. It was still cold but, it wasn't ice-cold.

Buddy then took my hands and put them in his. I could feel the heat rushing through my body, like water boiling in a kettle. Buddy began to shrink in size and my hands slipped away from him. I looked around and, I was back to my normal size while Buddy remained the same. I looked over at my brothers and, it was a little weird not seeing them in their elf-suits anymore. I went to look back at Buddy but, he was gone. He probably thought it would be easier to just leave rather than say goodbye. I went to the window and I could see this twinkle, like a star in the sky. I knew it was him and I waved to him. (*Goodbye, Buddy, my friend.*)

I slid into my bed, put on my pink woolly socks and slept like a baby. At around 11am, I woke to a banging noise. It was coming from the kitchen. I was still very tired from last night so, I didn't know if I was dreaming or, if Buddy had come back and was looking for the sugar. I sat up and wiped the sleep from my eyes. The boys were still fast asleep so, I knew it couldn't have been them. I crept out of bed slowly and reached for my dressing gown. I walked towards the kitchen door and caught a glimpse of brown wavy hair. It was Mammy. They were home. I got a sudden burst of energy and ran through the kitchen door. She was standing at the kitchen sink, filling the kettle for tea and Daddy was sitting at the table, reading a newspaper.

"Good morning, Shelia!" he called from behind his newspaper. I ran to him, gave him a big hug and welcomed him home.

"Good morning, Shelia, how is everything?" I ran over and gave my mother a big hug too.

"Ok love, calm down, I can't breathe."

"Oh, I'm sorry Mammy. I'm just so happy you're home safely. How was your trip to Dublin?"

"Very busy but, we're are sure glad to be home," Mammy replied with a sigh.

"It was chaos, you mean," Daddy joined in.

"A bunch of women fighting over Barbie dolls; it was ridiculous."

"Would you like some tea and breakfast? Sit down and I will make it," I said to them.

"Are you feeling okay there, Shelia? Maybe you need the doctor. You could have a fever?"

"No, I'm okay, Mammy. I just wanted to do something nice for you both after your long trip, that's all."

"Thank you, love, we have already eaten but, we wouldn't say no to a cuppa. The tea in Dublin was like stew; it was horrible."

"Oh, don't talk about stew, it will make me sick," I said, with that image of Liam getting sick still in my head.

"Oh! What happened?" Mammy asked, concerned as any mother naturally would be.

"Everything was okay but, Liam did happen to vomit on my lovely pink socks and then, Ronan went and slipped on it, hurting his back. Other than that and the cold weather, we were good."

"Well, it sounds like you handled the situation and your brothers very well, just as we expected."

"Thank you, Daddy ..." (Wait one minute, did he just say, "as we expected"? That sounded very suspicious.)

"Just one thing, Shelia love, where has the sugar gone?" Mammy asked, confused.

I knew she'd notice because the bag was nearly full when she left.

"Eh well, I went to make some warm milk last night for the boys and I accidently knocked it over into the sink. I'm sorry, I will replace it today."

"Not to worry, it's only sugar. Sure, we will have plenty of biscuits and cake over the Christmas?"

"Actually, Mammy, speaking of cakes and biscuits, I don't mind helping you make some for the parish hall."

She looked at me with amazement. "If you want to. I'll be delighted with the help."

"No problem at all," I replied happily.

Then she noticed something, something that I had totally forgotten about since last night.

"That's a pretty necklace you've got on, Shelia. Where did you get it?" she asked with curiosity.

Daddy barely lifted his head from the newspaper. This was a girl thing.

"Oh that!" I answered, acting as if I'd had it for ages.

"Eh, I got it ..." I put my hand on the necklace, closed my eyes and took a deep breath. I was just about to say, 'pound shop' when I heard a voice. It was Ronan. I was never so happy to see him.

"Morning, Kathleen, Dan, Queen of Sheba," he greeted everyone.

"Yep, it was Ronan and it sounded like he didn't remember anything about last night. He always addresses Mammy and Daddy by their first names. He thinks it makes him sound like an adult but, I think it makes him sound like an orphan. (*No, stop Shelia. I can't think like that anymore because I have to help him. I told Santa I would.*)

"How are things on the fields?" Daddy asked from behind the newspaper.

"Ticking over, still waiting for the calves," Ronan responded in true farmer talk.

"Very well. You did well."

Little did my father know how well Ronan had done in helping to rescue Santa. He was growing into a man.

"After your breakfast, we'll head out."

"No problem, Daddy, I'll get my boots on."

"Before any work gets done, sit down and eat," Mammy interrupted.

"Ok, Kathleen," Ronan replied.

Mammy cringes every time he calls her that but, she likes him to feel grown up so, she bites her tongue.

"I have a question to put to you. What happened last night?" (And now it's time to panic again.)

"Eh, what happened last night? What do you mean?" I asked back and I could feel the sweat running down my brow.

"When I checked on you all this morning, you were all fast asleep, like new-born babies and the room looked as if it was covered in glitter."

Oh no, maybe Buddy hadn't cleaned up as well as he could have done. What was I going to say? She was already suspicious of the necklace. You see, I don't ever wear jewellery so, she knew something was up.

"It was Shelia!" Ronan shouted.

"Eh, excuse me!" I shouted back.

"Shelia decided to tell us a Christmas story that was really boring so, then she got help from a friend at school and they turned the room into the North Pole."

"Really!" Mammy exclaimed.

Ronan then just finished stuffing his face and went out to the fields with Daddy.

"So, what do you know about the North Pole and who was this friend?" She asked like she was trying to read my mind.

"Well, what do you know about the North Pole?" I reflected the question back at her.

"Just what I've read about it," and she winked at me.

"The necklace?" she asked me again.

Did she know what I now knew or, was she trying to catch me out. I didn't want to expose Santa and Buddy. That's it; I got the answer.

"The necklace was an early birthday present from a buddy."

"Really!" She pretended that she believed what I was telling her.

Please, I knew she could read me like a book, she's my mother. She stared into my eyes. Neither of us blinked. Then she grinned at me and walked away.

"I thought maybe you got it from Aunt Helen. It would be more her style of jewellery."

Then, she walked off towards the bedrooms. Aunt Helen, of course, why didn't I think of that? Now she probably thought a boy gave it to me ... UGH! I screamed in my head. I could hear little voices coming from the bedroom. Liam and James were jumping on the beds, delighted to see Mammy of course.

"Did Shelia tell you a good bedtime story last night?" she continued to talk to the boys because she knew I was listening. Why couldn't she just let it go?

"It was getting to be a good story until she burned the milk, spilled the sugar and we all fell asleep waiting for her."

Mammy started to laugh hysterically.

"Presents! Presents!" James of course remembered that Mammy always brought home presents.

"Later boys, at lunch, okay."

"Ah!" they chorused back.

"Shelia, would you help me get the veggies from the shed."

"Yes, Mammy!" I answered from the door.

I hurried out and went to get the vegetables for lunch. I grabbed a head of cabbage, a bunch of carrots and a load of potatoes. My mouth was watering, thinking about this lovely, home-cooked meal that didn't contain candy canes or toffees.

Mammy prepared a delicious roast chicken, mash, shredded cabbage and cubed carrots. It was the best thing since sliced bread. After lunch mammy brought out the gifts.

"Books!" Ronan shouted with such sarcasm. "Great, another snooze-fest." He looked at me but, I resisted any banter this time.

Mammy used to be a teacher before she had us kids so, she loves books.

"Psst! Shelia, did you hear what I said?" Ronan whispered to me.

I just whispered back to him, "Hush!"

It left him speechless; I can tell you that. Mammy handed James a Christmas book and Liam got a book on superheroes. Then, Ronan's face was priceless. He got the thickest book of all. It was like a dictionary and encyclopaedia wrapped up in one. That's exactly what Ronan needed. When he opened it, there were no pages. It was a hollow box in the shape of a book. Inside, there was a bicycle repair kit.

"Why do I need this?" Ronan was totally clueless.

"Did you have a good look inside Ronan?" Ronan rooted round the box and found a photo of (Would you believe it?) a mountain bike. He held the picture up and had a good look.

"Is this what I think it is?" He asked, now with expectation and hope.

"Mr Connors is delivering it from the shop tomorrow," Daddy told a stunned Ronan.

"Snooze-fest is it?" I whispered back to Ronan, who I think could only hear the word bike.

"Thank you, Daddy. Thank you, Mammy. It's the best gift ever!"

"Well that's for your sixteenth so, don't go getting any other ideas," Mammy warned him.

"I will go out and see if we have a lock for it." Ronan was delighted.

"Don't think we have forgotten about you," Mammy looked at me.

"I don't mind. Whatever you give me, I am very grateful.

"Ok, where has Shelia gone?" Mammy asked sarcastically.

"Nowhere, it's really me," I assured her.

"Ok, well, I saw this and thought of you. I can take it back if you don't like it. It's a book about Florence Nightingale. She was a nurse in the olden days and this is also for you."

She gave me a little blue box, tied up with a white ribbon. I opened it slowly and gasped when I saw what was inside. A beautiful gold watch with an engraving on the back which said, "Happy 16th Birthday".

"Wow, it is absolutely gorgeous. Thank you, Mammy and Daddy."

"You're welcome love. I'm glad you like it."

I helped Mammy clean away the plates and saucepans after lunch. We stood side by side. She washed while I dried up and put the dishes away. The kitchen was very silent. The boys were watching TV. Ronan and Daddy had gone out to the yard. All you could hear was the clattering of plates and banging of presses. I then plucked up the courage to ask her.

“Mammy, what was your mother like?”

“Crazy!” Mammy replied sharply.

“Why would you say that?” I continued.

“Oh sorry, love. I didn’t mean for that to sound like a bad thing. She was a very happy mum; she just told a lot of crazy stories. She could have written many books and filled a library.”

“Did you not believe her stories?” I kept probing.

“It’s not that I didn’t believe them. It’s just that there were a lot of them. It was hard to keep up. She even repeated them after she became ill.”

“Do you remember any? I would love to hear some.”

“Ok, did you and James swap brains overnight? It’s not like you to be caught up in fairy tales.”

Well, I suppose she is my mother and she knew I was acting strange.

“No, I’m perfectly fine, honestly. I was just thinking of Nana, that’s all!”

“Well, alright then, let me think of a good one. Oh yeah. There was one I used to truly believe when I was a little girl.”

“Go on, I’m listening.”

We were both sitting at the kitchen table now. I was filled with anticipation.

"So, one Christmas Eve, when I was about six years old, she told me a story about going to help Santa and his elves in the North Pole. She claimed that Santa had sent for her personally to come and help him find his 'naughty or nice' list."

"And what happened when she was there?" I started to get excited.

"It was something like, Santa helped her to truly believe in Christmas and she helped him find 'The List'.

"Oh my," I started to get shivers down my spine while I was listening to my mother speak. She looked at me strangely.

"It's only a story, Shelia."

"Yeah, of course, I know that but, it sounds like a really magical one."

"Yeah well, that's mammies for you," she said and gave me a wink.

She knew, I knew but, neither of us could talk about it.

"Shelia! Shelia! Tell us a story!" James said, as he came bursting into the kitchen and nearly hitting his head off the corner of the table so, I grabbed him tightly.

Mammy smiled and pretended to be doing housework.

"Sure, what would I know about stories?" I answered back, knowing that she was listening.

"Why don't you finish the one you started last night? I promise I won't fall asleep this time."

"Just make it a little more exciting," said Liam, coming in the door behind him.

"Oh! It's exciting you want?"

Both of them nodded.

"Alright. Everyone around the table," I called out.

"Does that include me?" Mammy asked, joining in the fun.

"Especially you. There will be a little something for everyone in this story."

"Oh well, you can definitely count me in. I'll just put on the kettle and we can have some tea and biscuits. Mammy hung up her apron and got out the biscuit tin.

"It was a very cold winter and there was trouble brewing in the North Pole. Freddy Freeze, a grumpy elf was up to no good ..."

EPILOGUE

It was a cold, damp Christmas morning. The rain from last night had stopped so people could attend their annual Christmas Day Mass. I woke up feeling a bit cold but luckily, we hadn't had an icy day since I had made my trip to the North Pole. This was going to be a magical Christmas. I could feel it. Not only did I have an out of this world Christmas experience but today, I was turning sixteen. I was almost an adult but, I still felt a bit like a child that day. Santa had come and left us all something special.

"Shelia! Shelia! Get up, it's Christmas!" James was screaming at the top of his voice.

There was no doubt that he was going to have a sore throat the next day. I pulled back my bed covers and put my feet on the floor. I looked down. Two woolly socks? Check. I reached for my dressing gown and followed the rather hyper elf down the hall to the sittingroom. Mammy was already up and working her magic in the kitchen. The delicious smell of turkey and ham was spreading throughout the house. It just hit you in the face, like the smell of the warm apple pie with custard that Mammy makes every week for dessert. She likes to have the heavy work done before Liam and James wake up or, she will get nothing done.

I went into the kitchen first and wished her a Happy Christmas. She gave me a hug and asked if the boys were up.

"Like two jack-in-the-boxes," I replied.

She cleaned her hands and we both went to the sittingroom. And there she stood, our beautiful, stick-like Christmas tree. There were red and green baubles hanging on the pineless branches. Tinsel and fairy lights were draped around her stick body and a big gold star at the top, like a crown.

Yep! There she was, our traditional pineless tree with lots of pressies.

"Can we open them? Can we? Can we?" James was shouting while Liam was just kneeling down in front of them in a trance.

"Whoa there, what's all the fuss about?" Daddy came in.

"Santa came. He was here, Daddy," James shouted with excitement.

"Oh, is there anything for me?"

"No, silly Daddy, you're too big. You don't play with toys anymore," said James.

Ronan then came barging in, rubbing his eyes. "What's with all the yelling about? People are trying to sleep."

"People, what people, everyone I know is awake," I answered back.

Ronan looked at me and grinned. "I knew the Queen of Sheba was there somewhere."

I picked up a present I had wrapped for him.

"Ah Shelia! You shouldn't have," he replied with a hint of sarcasm.

(Yes, Ronan and Shelia were back to normal.)

Daddy and James were still deep in conversation about who was and wasn't entitled to Santa's presents.

"If I'm too big, as you say, why is there a giant box over there? Surely that one is for me?"

James gasped. His eyes widened. This was a rather large box. The lid was like the lid on a shoebox. The wrapping paper was red and it had a white bow on top. It's not the usual Christmas wrapping we were used to but, hey, I'm not going to question the elves on poor choice of wrapping. This particular box did seem unusual.

"How do we decide who gets to open it?" Daddy asked.

"Let's check the label," Mammy said.

"To The O'Reilly Family. I hope you have a joyful Christmas. From Santa."

"Wow, Daddy, it's for everyone," James said.

"Let's all open it together. Everyone gather around and, on the count of three, lift," Mammy gave the orders.

"Ronan, aren't you going to join us?"

"Ah Ma, why?" Ronan, of course, was being Mr Scrooge.

"Ronan!" Mammy gave him the do-as-I-say look. Ronan got up, left the gift on the chair and slowly walked across the room.

"Ok, everyone, on my count ... one, two and ... three!"

We all gasped as we looked into the mysterious box that Santa had left. There he was. White, fluffy, dark eyes, peach nose and bushy tail. It was our very own bunny rabbit. He was beautiful. I even think Ronan fell in love. Once you saw those eyes and whiskers, he melted your heart.

"Aren't you going to hold him?" said Mammy. Ronan, of course, was the first one in, like an elf to sugar.

"Eh, I was talking to the smaller ones ..." Mammy was just about to say but, she stopped.

"Oh wow, we got our very own rabbit," James said, whilst jumping up and down and clapping his hands.

"Can I hold him next?"

"Then I'm after you, James," Liam finally spoke after the surprise he had got.

"Can he stay in my bed?" Liam asked.

"No!" both Mammy and Daddy replied sharply.

"Ronan can make a pen for him out in the barn," said Daddy.

"But he might get lonely," James said sorrowfully.

"How can he get lonely when there are loads of animals outside? He will feel at home around his own kind," Daddy tried to reassure him.

"Why don't you feed him some lettuce from the kitchen?"

"Yeah! Let's go, James." Liam went straight out to get some.

"I'll go and get the pen ready," said Ronan.

"Hold on, everybody!" I decided to get my share of the excitement.

"We haven't picked a name for him."

"What about Ronan the Rabbit?" (Typical Ronan.)

Then I suggested, "What about Buddy?"

"You mean, like the elf in your story?" Liam remembered.

"Yeah, that's way better than Ronan," James agreed.

So, it was settled. Buddy was officially a new member of the O'Reilly family.

"Are we all finished up here now only, Buddy does need a home before my Christmas dinner?" said Ronan. Just when I thought Ronan was all heart.

Now, it was my turn to complete Santa's request. I noticed Ronan was heading straight out to the barn so, I grabbed the present I had gotten for him. I put on my coat and wellies and followed him.

It was dull and damp outside.

"Ronan! Ronan! Wait up!" I called after him. He stopped and walked back towards me.

"Yeah, what's up?"

"The present I gave you, open it, eh, please?"

"Is that all?" (I looked up at the sky and thought, *Give me patience.*)

"Just open it!"

Inside, I was kind of smiling and wishing I had a camera to take a picture of his face. Ronan tore open the present and his face was priceless.

"Ah Shelia! I thought you were only joking about the pink socks."

I let him squirm for a few minutes whilst I laughed my head off.

"Quick, Shelia, take them back inside before someone sees them." He was pleading with me.

"Relax, Ronan, they're not for you to wear. They're called novelty socks. I want you to give them to Jenny Murphy as a present from you."

"Why would I want to do that?" Ronan started to blush.

"Because the Queen of Sheba told you to. Now, go on."

"But what about Buddy and the pen?" he said, delaying.

"He'll be fine. Besides, Liam and James won't let him out of their sight."

"But what will I say?" he started getting anxious.

"Well, I don't know. That's why I gave you the socks. Conversation starter and all that. Seriously, Ronan, give it a shot. What's the worst that can happen?"

"She might say, 'get lost'!" Ronan said, exaggerating.

"Or she might appreciate the thought," I said.

"Ronan, don't be afraid, you're one of the good guys."

Then, with those words, he left, whistling and skipping down the road. I smiled at him as he disappeared into the distance. I looked up at the dull grey sky and light snowflakes began to fall. I called out to Santa, "Happy Christmas, you owe me one!"

I wrapped my coat around me tightly, pulled up my hood and I went back inside.

The End